John Ruskin

The Crown of Wild Olive

Three Lectures on Work, Traffic and War

John Ruskin

The Crown of Wild Olive
Three Lectures on Work, Traffic and War

ISBN/EAN: 9783337269661

Printed in Europe, USA, Canada, Australia, Japan

Cover: Foto ©Andreas Hilbeck / pixelio.de

More available books at **www.hansebooks.com**

THE

CROWN OF WILD OLIVE.

Three Lectures

ON

WORK, TRAFFIC, AND WAR.

BY

JOHN RUSKIN, M.A.

'And indeed it should have been of gold, had not Jupiter been so poor.'
ARISTOPHANES (*Plutus*).

NEW YORK:
JOHN WILEY & SON,
15 ASTOR PLACE.
1874.

PREFACE.

TWENTY YEARS ago, there was no lovelier piece of lowland scenery in South England, nor any more pathetic in the world, by its expression of sweet human character and life, than that immediately bordering on the sources of the Wandle, and including the lower moors of Addington, and the villages of Beddington and Carshalton, with all their pools and streams. No clearer or diviner waters ever sang with constant lips of the hand which 'giveth rain from heaven;' no pastures ever lightened in spring time with more passionate blossoming; no sweeter homes ever hallowed the heart of the passer-by with their pride of peaceful gladness—fain-hidden—yet full-confessed. The place remains, or, until a few months ago, remained, nearly unchanged in its larger features; but, with deliberate mind I say, that I have never seen anything so ghastly in its inner tragic meaning,—not in Pisan Maremma,—not by Campagna tomb,—not by the sand-isles of the Torcellan shore,—as the slow stealing of aspects of reckless, indolent, animal neglect, over the delicate sweetness of that English

scene : nor is any blasphemy or impiety—any frantic saying
or godless thought—more appalling to me, using the best
power of judgment I have to discern its sense and scope,
than the insolent defilings of those springs by the human
herds that drink of them.   Just where the welling of stainless water, trembling and pure, like a body of light, enters
the pool of Carshalton, cutting itself a radiant channel down
to the gravel, through warp of feathery weeds, all waving,
which it traverses with its deep threads of clearness, like
the chalcedony in moss-agate, starred here and there with
white grenouillette; just in the very rush and murmur of
the first spreading currents, the human wretches of the
place cast their street and house foulness; heaps of dust and
slime, and broken shreds of old metal, and rags of putrid
clothes; they having neither energy to cart it away, nor
decency enough to dig it into the ground, thus shed into
the stream, to diffuse what venom of it will float and melt,
far away, in all places where God meant those waters to
bring joy and health.   And, in a little pool, behind some
houses farther in the village, where another spring rises, the
shattered stones of the well, and of the little fretted channel
which was long ago built and traced for it by gentler
hands, lie scattered, each from each, under a ragged bank
of mortar, and scoria; and bricklayers' refuse, on one side,
which the clean water nevertheless chastises to purity ; but

it cannot conquer the dead earth beyond ; and there, circled and coiled under festering scum, the stagnant edge of the pool effaces itself into a slope of black slime, the accumulation of indolent years. Half-a-dozen men, with one day's work, could cleanse those pools, and trim the flowers about their banks, and make every breath of summer air above them rich with cool balm ; and every glittering wave medicinal, as if it ran, troubled of angels, from the porch of Bethesda. But that day's work is never given, nor will be ; nor will any joy be possible to heart of man, for evermore, about those wells of English waters.

When I last left them, I walked up slowly through the back streets of Croydon, from the old church to the hos· pital ; and, just on the left, before coming up to the crossing of the High Street, there was a new public-house built. And the front of it was built in so wise manner, that a recess of two feet was left below its front windows, between them and the street-pavement—a recess too narrow for any possible use (for even if it had been occupied by a seat, as in old time it might have been, everybody walking along the street would have fallen over the legs of the reposing wayfarers). But, by way of making this two feet depth of freehold land more expressive of the dignity of an establishment for the sale of spirituous liquors, it was fenced from the pavement by an imposing iron railing, having fou*

or five spearheads to the yard of it, and six feet high; containing as much iron and iron-work, indeed, as could well
be put into the space ; and by this stately arrangement, the
little piece of dead ground within, between wall and street,
became a protective receptacle of refuse; cigar ends, and
oyster shells, and the like, such as an open-handed English
street-populace habitually scatters from its presence, and
was thus left, unsweepable by any ordinary methods. Now
the iron bars which, uselessly (or in great degree worse
than uselessly), enclosed this bit of ground, and made it
pestilent, represented a quantity of work which would have
cleansed the Carshalton pools three times over;—of work,
partly cramped and deadly, in the mine; partly fierce* and

---

* 'A fearful occurrence took place a few days since, near Wolverhamp-
ton. Thomas Snape, aged nineteen, was on duty as the "keeper" of a
blast furnace at Deepfield, assisted by John Gardner, aged eighteen, and
Joseph Swift, aged thirty-seven. The furnace contained four tons of molten
iron, and an equal amount of cinders, and ought to have been run out at 7-30
P.M. But Snape and his mates, engaged in talking and drinking, neglected
their duty, and, in the meantime, the iron rose in the furnace until it reached
a pipe wherein water was contained. Just as the men had stripped, and
were proceeding to tap the furnace, the water in the pipe, converted into
steam, burst down its front and let loose on them the molten metal, which
instantaneously consumed Gardner; Snape, terribly burnt, and mad with
pain, leaped into the canal and then ran home and fell dead on the threshold, Swift survived to reach the hospital, where he died too.'

exhaustive, at the furnace ; partly foolish and sedentary, of ill-taught students making bad designs : work from the beginning to the last fruits of it, and in all the branches of it, venomous, deathful, and miserable. Now, how did it come to pass that this work was done instead of the other; that the strength and life of the English operative were spent in defiling ground, instead of redeeming it; and in producing an entirely (in that place) valueless piece of metal, which can neither be eaten nor breathed; instead of medicinal fresh air, and pure water ?

There is but one reason for it, and at present a conclusive one,—that the capitalist can charge per-centage on the work in the one case, and cannot in the other. If, having certain funds for supporting labour at my disposal, I pay men merely to keep my ground in order, my money is, in that function, spent once for all ; but if I pay them to dig iron out of my ground, and work it, and sell it, I can charge rent for the ground, and per-centage both on the manufacture and the sale, and make my capital profitable in these three bye-ways. The greater part of the profitable invest-ment of capital, in the present day, is in operations of this

In further illustration of this matter, I beg the reader to look at the article on the 'Decay of the English Race,' in the 'Pall-Mall Gazette' of April 17, of this year; and at the articles on the 'Report of the Thames Commission,' in any journals of the same date.

kind, in which the public is persuaded to buy something
of no use to it, on production, or sale, of which, the capitalist may charge per-centage; the said public remaining all
the while under the persuasion that the per centages thus
obtained are real national gains, whereas, they are merely
filchings out of partially light pockets, to swell heavy
ones.

Thus, the Croydon publican buys the iron railing, to
make himself more conspicuous to drunkards. The public-
house-keeper on the other side of the way presently buys
another railing, to out-rail him with. Both are, as to their
relative attractiveness to customers of taste, just where they
were before; but they have lost the price of the railings;
which they must either themselves finally lose, or make
their aforesaid customers of taste pay, by raising the price
of their beer, or adulterating it. Either the publicans, or
their customers, are thus poorer by precisely what the
capitalist has gained; and the value of the work itself,
meantime, has been lost to the nation; the iron bars in
that form and place being wholly useless. It is this mode
of taxation of the poor by the rich which is referred to in
the text (page 31), in comparing the modern acquisitive
power of capital with that of the lance and sword; the
only difference being that the levy of black mail in old
times was by force, and is now by cozening. The old

rider and reiver frankly quartered himself on the publican .
for the night; the modern one merely makes his lance into
an iron spike, and persuades his host to buy it. One
comes as an open robber, the other as a cheating pedlar;
but the result, to the injured person's pocket, is absolutely
the same. Of course many useful industries mingle with,
and disguise the useless ones; and in the habits of energy
aroused by the struggle, there is a certain direct good. It
is far better to spend four thousand pounds in making a
good gun, and then to blow it to pieces, than to pass life
in idleness. Only do not let it be called 'political economy.'
There is also a confused notion in the minds of many persons, that the gathering of the property of the poor into
the hands of the rich does no ultimate harm; since, in
whosesoever hands it may be, it must be spent at last, and
thus, they think, return to the poor again. This fallacy
has been again and again exposed; but grant the plea true,
and the same apology may, of course, be made for black
mail, or any other form of robbery. It might be (though
practically it never is) as advantageous for the nation that
the robber should have the spending of the money he ex-
torts, as that the person robbed should have spent it. But
this is no excuse for the theft. If I were to put a turnpike
on the road where it passes my own gate, and endeavour
to exact a shilling from every passenger, the public would

soon do away with my gate, without listening to any plea
on my part that 'it was as advantageous to them, in the
end, that I should spend their shillings, as that they themselves should.' But if, instead of out-facing them with a
turnpike, I can only persuade them to come in and buy
stones, or old iron, or any other useless thing, out of my
ground, I may rob them to the same extent, and be, more-
over, thanked as a public benefactor, and promoter of com
mercial prosperity. And this main question for the poor
of England—for the poor of all countries—is wholly
omitted in every common treatise on the subject of wealth.
Even by the labourers themselves, the operation of capital
is regarded only in its effect on their immediate interests;
never in the far more terrific power of its appointment of
the kind and the object of labour. It matters little, ultimately, how much a labourer is paid for making anything;
but it matters fearfully what the thing is, which he is com-
pelled to make. If his labour is so ordered as to produce
food, and fresh air, and fresh water, no matter that his
wages are low;—the food and fresh air and water will be
at last there; and he will at last get them. But if he is
paid to destroy food and fresh air, or to produce iron bars
instead of them,—the food and air will finally *not* be there,
and he will *not* get them, to his great and final incon-
venience. So that, conclusively, in political as in house-

hold economy, the great question is, not so much what money you have in your pocket, as what you will buy with it, and do with it.

I have been long accustomed, as all men engaged in work of investigation must be, to hear my statements laughed at for years, before they are examined or believed; and I am generally content to wait the public's time. But it has not been without displeased surprise that I have found myself totally unable, as yet, by any repetition, or illustration, to force this plain thought into my readers' heads,—that the wealth of nations, as of men, consists in substance, not in ciphers; and that the real good of all work, and of all commerce, depends on the final worth of the thing you make, or get by it. This is a practical enough statement, one would think: but the English public has been so possessed by its modern school of economists with the notion that Business is always good, whether it be busy in mischief or in benefit; and that buying and selling are always salutary, whatever the intrinsic worth of what you buy or sell,—that it seems impossible to gain so much as a patient hearing for any inquiry respecting the substantial result of our eager modern labours. I have never felt more checked by the sense of this impossibility than in arranging the heads of the following three lectures, which, though delivered at con-

siderable intervals of time, and in different places, were
not prepared without reference to each other. Their connection would, however, have been made far more distinct,
if I had not been prevented, by what I feel to be another
great difficulty in addressing English audiences, from enforcing, with any decision, the common, and to me the most important, part of their subjects. I chiefly desired (as I have
just said) to question my hearers—operatives, merchants,
and soldiers, as to the ultimate meaning of the *business* they
had in hand; and to know from them what they expected
or intended their manufacture to come to, their selling to
come to, and their killing to come to. That appeared the
first point needing determination before I could speak to
them with any real utility or effect. 'You craftsmen—sales-
men—swordsmen,—do but tell me clearly what you want,
then, if I can say anything to help you, I will; and if not, I
will account to you as I best may for my inability.' But
in order to put this question into any terms, one had first
of all to face the difficulty just spoken of—to me for the
present insuperable,—the difficulty of knowing whether to
address one's audience as believing, or not believing, in
any other world than this. For if you address any average
modern English company as believing in an Eternal life,
and endeavour to draw any conclusions, from this assumed
belief, as to their present business, they will forthwith tell

you that what you say is very beautiful, but it is not practical. If, on the contrary, you frankly address them as unbelievers in Eternal life, and try to draw any con-sequences from that unbelief,—they immediately hold you for an accursed person, and shake off the dust from their feet at you. And the more I thought over what I had got to say, the less I found I could say it, without some refer-ence to this intangible or intractable part of the subject. It made all the difference, in asserting any principle of war, whether one assumed that a discharge of artillery would merely knead down a certain quantity of red clay into a level line, as in a brick field; or whether, out of every separately Christian-named portion of the ruinous heap, there went out, into the smoke and dead-fallen air of battle, some astonished condition of soul, unwillingly released. It made all the difference, in speaking of the possible range of commerce, whether one assumed that all bargains re-lated only to visible property—or whether property, for the present invisible, but nevertheless real, was elsewhere purchaseable on other terms. It made all the difference, in addressing a body of men subject to considerable hard-ship, and having to find some way out of it—whether one could confidently say to them, 'My friends,—you have only to die, and all will be right;' or whether one had any secret misgiving that such advice was more blessed to him that gave, than to him that took it. And therefore the deliberate reader will find, throughout these lectures, a hesitation in driving points home, and a pausing short of conclusions which he will feel I would fain have come to; hesitation which arises wholly from this uncertainty of my hearers' temper. For I do not now speak, nor have I ever spoken, since the time of first forward youth, in any prose lyting temper, as desiring to persuade any one of what, in such matters, I thought myself; but, whomsoever I venture to address, I take for the time his creed as I find it; and endeavour to push it into such vital fruit as it seems capable of. Thus, it is a creed with a great part of the existing English people, that they are in possession of a book which tells them, straight from the lips of God all they ought to do, and need to know. I have read that book, with as much care as most of them, for some forty years; and am thankful that, on those who trust it, I can press its pleadings. My endeavour has been uniformly to make them trust it more deeply than they do; trust it, not in their own favourite verses only, but in the sum of all; trust it not as a fetish or talisman, which they are to be saved by daily repetitions of; but as a Captain's order, to be heard and obeyed at their peril. I was always encouraged by supposing my hearers to hold such belief. To these, if to any, I once had hope of addressing, with acceptance, words which insisted on the guilt of pride, and the futility of avarice; from these, if from any, I once expected ratification of a political economy, which asserted that the life was more than the meat, and the body than raiment; and these, it once seemed to me, I might ask, without accusation of fanaticism, not merely in doctrine of the lips, but in the bestowal of their heart's treasure, to separate themselves from the crowd of whom it is written, ' After all these things do the Gentiles seek.'

It cannot, however, be assumed, with any semblance of reason, that a general audience is now wholly, or even in majority, composed of these religious persons. A large portion must always consist of men who admit no such creed; or who, at least, are inaccessible to appeals founded on it. And as, with the so-called Christian, I desired to plead for honest declaration and fulfilment of his belief in life,—with the so-called Infidel, I desired to plead for an honest declaration and fulfilment of his belief in death. The dilemma is inevitable. Men must either hereafter live, or hereafter die; fate may be bravely met, and conduct wisely ordered, on either expectation; but never in hesitation between ungrasped hope, and unconfronted fear. We usually believe in immortality, so far as to avoid preparation for death; and in mortality, so far as to avoid preparation for anything after death. Whereas, a wise man will at least hold himself prepared for one or other of two events, of which one or other is inevitable; and will have all things in order, for his sleep, or in readiness, for his awakening.

Nor have we any right to call it an ignoble judgment, if he determine to put them in order, as for sleep. A brave belief in life is indeed an enviable state of mind, but, as far as I can discern, an unusual one. I know few Christians so convinced of the splendour of the rooms in their Father's house, as to be happier when their friends are called to those mansions, than they would have been if the Queen had sent for them to live at court: nor has the Church's most ardent 'desire to depart, and be with Christ,' ever cured it of the singular habit of putting on mourning for every person summoned to such departure. On the contrary, a brave belief in death has been assuredly held by many not ignoble persons, and it is a sign of the last depravity in the Church itself, when it assumes that such a belief is inconsistent with either purity of character, or energy of hand. The shortness of life is not, to any rational person, a conclusive reason for wasting the space of it which may be granted him; nor does the anticipation of death to-morrow suggest, to any one but a drunkard, the expediency of drunkenness to-day. To teach that there is no device in the grave, may indeed make the deviceless person more contented in his dullness;

but it will make the deviser only more earnest in devising:
nor is human conduct likely, in every case, to be purer,
under the conviction that all its evil may in a moment be
pardoned, and all its wrong-doing in a moment redeemed;
and that the sigh of repentance, which purges the guilt
of the past, will waft the soul into a felicity which forgets
its pain,—than it may be under the sterner, and to many
not unwise minds, more probable, apprehension, that
'what a man soweth that shall he also reap'—or others
reap,—when he, the living seed of pestilence, walketh no
more in darkness, but lies down therein.

But to men whose feebleness of sight, or bitterness of
soul, or the offence given by the conduct of those who
claim higher hope, may have rendered this painful creed
the only possible one, there is an appeal to be made, more
secure in its ground than any which can be addressed to
happier persons. I would fain, if I might offencelessly,
have spoken to them as if none others heard; and have
said thus: Hear me, you dying men, who will soon be
deaf for ever. For these others, at your right hand and
your left, who look forward to a state of infinite existence,
in which all their errors will be overruled, and all their
faults forgiven; for these, who, stained and blackened in
the battle smoke of mortality, have but to dip themselves
for an instant in the font of death, and to rise renewed of

plumage, as a dove that is covered with silver, and her feathers like gold; for these, indeed, it may be permissible to waste their numbered moments, through faith in a future of innumerable hours; to these, in their weakness, it may be conceded that they should tamper with sin which can only bring forth fruit of righteousness, and profit by the iniquity which, one day, will be remembered no more. In them, it may be no sign of hardness of heart to neglect the poor, over whom they know their Master is watching; and to leave those to perish temporarily, who cannot perish eternally. But, for you, there is no such hope, and therefore no such excuse. This fate, which you ordain for the wretched, you believe to be all their inheritance; you may crush them, before the moth, and they will never rise to rebuke you;—their breath, which fails for lack of food, once expiring, will never be recalled to whisper against you a word of accusing;—they and you, as you think, shall lie down together in the dust, and the worms cover you;—and for them there shall be no consolation, and on you no vengeance,— only the question murmured above your grave: 'Who shall repay him what he hath done?' Is it therefore easier for you in your heart to inflict the sorrow for which there is no remedy? Will you take, wantonly, this little all of his life from your poor brother, and make his brief

hours long to him with pain? Will you be readier to
the injustice which can never be redressed; and niggardly of
mercy which you *can* bestow but once, and which, refusing,
you refuse for ever? I think better of you, even of the
most selfish, than that you would do this, well understood.
And for yourselves, it seems to me, the question becomes
not less grave, in these curt limits. If your life were but a
fever fit,—the madness of a night, whose follies were all to
be forgotten in the dawn, it might matter little how you
fretted away the sickly hours,—what toys you snatched at,
or let fall,—what visions you followed wistfully with the
deceived eyes of sleepless phrenzy. Is the earth only an
hospital? Play, if you care to play, on the floor of the
hospital dens. Knit its straw into what crowns please you;
gather the dust of it for treasure, and die rich in that,
clutching at the black motes in the air with your dying
hands;—and yet, it may be well with you. But if this life
be no dream, and the world no hospital; if all the peace and
power and joy you can ever win, must be won now; and
all fruit of victory gathered here, or never;—will you still,
throughout the puny totality of your life, weary yourselves
in the fire for vanity? If there is no rest which remain-
eth for you, is there none you might presently take? was
this grass of the earth made green for your shroud only,
not for your bed? and can you never lie down *upon* it, but

only *under* it?   The heathen, to whose creed you have returned, thought not so.   They knew that life brought its contest, but they expected from it also the crown of all contest: No proud one! no jewelled circlet flaming through Heaven above the height of the unmerited throne; only some few leaves of wild olive, cool to the tired brow, through a few years of peace.   It should have been of gold, they thought; but Jupiter was poor; this was the best the god could give them.   Seeking a greater than this, they had known it a mockery.   Not in war, not in wealth, not in tyranny, was there any happiness to be found for them—only in kindly peace, fruitful and free. The wreath was to be of *wild* olive, mark you :—the tree that grows carelessly, tufting the rocks with no vivid bloom, no verdure of branch ; only with soft snow of blossom, and scarcely fulfilled fruit, mixed with grey leaf and thorn-set stem; no fastening of diadem for you but with such sharp embroidery !   But this, such as it is, you may win while yet you live; type of grey honour and sweet rest.* Free-heartedness, and graciousness, and undisturbed trust, and requited love, and the sight of the peace of others, and the ministry to their pain ;—these, and the blue sky above you, and the sweet waters and flowers of the earth beneath ;

* μελιτόεσσα, ἀέθλων γ' ἕνεκεν.

and mysteries and presences, innumerable, of living things, —these may yet be here your riches; untormenting and divine: serviceable for the life that now is; nor, it may be, without promise of that which is to come.

CONTENTS.

——o——

LECTURE I.

LECTURE II.

LECTURE III.

WORK.

LECTURE I.

WORK.

(Delivered before the Working Men's Institute, at Camberwell.)

MY FRIENDS,—I have not come among you to-night to
endeavour to give you an entertaining lecture; but to tell you
a few plain facts, and ask you some plain, but necessary
questions. I have seen and known too much of the struggle
for life among our labouring population, to feel at ease, even
under any circumstances, in inviting them to dwell on the
trivialities of my own studies; but, much more, as I meet to-
night, for the first time, the members of a working Institute
established in the district in which I have passed the greater
part of my life, I am desirous that we should at once understand each other, on graver matters. I would fain tell you,
with what feelings, and with what hope, I regard this Insti-
tution, as one of many such, now happily established throughout England, as well as in other countries;—Institutions
which are preparing the way for a great change in all the
circumstances of industrial life; but of which the success
must wholly depend upon our clearly understanding the cir-

cumstances and necessary *limits* of this change. No teacher
can truly promote the cause of education, until he knows the
conditions of the life for which that education is to prepare
his pupil. And the fact that he is called upon to address
you, nominally, as a 'Working Class,' must compel him, if
he is in any wise earnest or thoughtful, to enquire in the outset, on what you yourselves suppose this class distinction has
been founded in the past, and must be founded in the future.
The manner of the amusement, and the matter of the teaching, which any of us can offer you, must depend wholly on
our first understanding from you, whether you think the
distinction heretofore drawn between working men and
others, is truly or falsely founded. Do you accept it as it
stands? do you wish it to be modified? or do you think the
object of education is to efface it, and make us forget it for
ever?

Let me make myself more distinctly understood. We call
this—you and I—a 'Working Men's' Institute, and our college in London, a 'Working Men's' College. Now, how do
you consider that these several institutes differ, or ought to
differ, from 'idle men's' institutes and 'idle men's' colleges?
Or by what other word than 'idle' shall I distinguish those
whom the happiest and wisest of working men do not object
to call the 'Upper Classes?' Are there really upper
classes,—are there lower? How much should they always

be elevated, how much always depressed? And, gentlemen and ladies—I pray those of you who are here to forgive me the offence there may be in what I am going to say. It is not *I* who wish to say it. Bitter voices say it; voices of battle and of famine through all the world, which must be heard some day, whoever keeps silence. Neither is it to *you* specially that I say it. I am sure that most now present know their duties of kindness, and fulfil them, better perhaps than I do mine. But I speak to you as representing your whole class, which errs, I know, chiefly by thoughtlessness, but not therefore the less terribly. Wilful error is limited by the will, but what limit is there to that of which we are unconscious?

Bear with me, therefore, while I turn to these workmen, and ask them, also as representing a great multitude, what they think the 'upper classes' are, and ought to be, in relation to them. Answer, you workmen who are here, as you would among yourselves, frankly; and tell me how you would have me call those classes. Am I to call them—would *you* think me right in calling them—the idle classes? I think you would feel somewhat uneasy, and as if I were not treating my subject honestly, or speaking from my heart, if I went on under the supposition that all rich people were idle. You would be both unjust and unwise if you allowed me to say that;—not less unjust than the rich people who say that all the poor are idle, and will never work if they can help it, or more than they can help.

For indeed the fact is, that there are idle poor and idle rich; and there are busy poor and busy rich. Many a beggar is as lazy as if he had ten thousand a year; and many a man of large fortune is busier than his errand-boy, and never would think of stopping in the street to play marbles. So that, in a large view, the distinction between workers and idlers, as between knaves and honest men, runs through the very heart and innermost economies of men of all ranks and in all positions. There is a working class—strong and happy—among both rich and poor; there is an idle class— weak, wicked, and miserable—among both rich and poor. And the worst of the misunderstandings arising between the two orders come of the unlucky fact that the wise of one class habitually contemplate the foolish of the other. If the busy rich people watched and rebuked the idle rich people, all would be right; and if the busy poor people watched and rebuked the idle poor people, all would be right. But each class has a tendency to look for the faults of the other. A hard-working man of property is particularly offended by an idle beggar; and an orderly, but poor, workman is naturally intolerant of the licentious luxury of the rich. And what is severe judgment in the minds of the just men of either class, becomes fierce enmity in the unjust—but among the unjust *only.* None but the dissolute among the poor look upon the rich as their natural enemies, or desire to pillage their houses and divide their property. None but the dissolute among the rich speak in opprobrious terms of the vices and follies of the poor.

There is, then, no class distinction between idle and industrious people; and I am going to-night to speak only of the industrious. The idle people we will put out of our thoughts at once—they are mere nuisances—what ought to be done with *them*, we'll talk of at another time. But there are class distinctions among the industrious themselves;—tremendous distinctions, which rise and fall to every degree in the infinite thermometer of human pain and of human power—distinctions of high and low, of lost and won, to the whole reach of man's soul and body.

These separations we will study, and the laws of them, among energetic men only, who, whether they work or whether they play, put their strength into the work, and their strength into the game; being in the full sense of the word 'industrious,' one way or another— with a purpose, or without. And these distinctions are mainly **four:**

I. Between those who work, and those who play.

II. Between those who produce the means of life, and those who consume them.

III. Between those who work with the head, and those who work with the hand.

IV. Between those who work wisely, and who work foolishly.

For easier memory, let us say we are going to oppose, in our examination,—

   I. Work to play;

   II. Production to consumption;

   III. Head to hand; and,

   IV. Sense to nonsense.

I. First, then, of the distinction between the classes who work and the classes who play. Of course we must agree upon a definition of these terms,—work and play,—before going farther. Now, roughly, not with vain subtlety of definition, but for plain use of the words, 'play' is an exertion of body or mind, made to please ourselves, and with no determined end; and work is a thing done because it ought to be done, and with a determined end. You play, as you call it, at cricket, for-instance. That is as hard work as anything else; but it amuses you, and it has no result but the amusement. If it were done as an ordered form of exercise, for health's sake, it would become work directly. So, in like manner, whatever we do to please ourselves, and only for the sake of the pleasure, not for an ultimate object, is 'play,' the 'pleasing thing,' not the useful thing. Play may be useful

in a secondary sense (nothing is indeed more useful or necessary); but the use of it depends on its being spontaneous.

Let us, then, enquire together what sort of games the playing class in England spend their lives in playing at.

The first of all English games is making money. That is
an all-absorbing game; and we knock each other down oftener in playing at that than at foot-ball, or any other roughest
sport; and it is absolutely without purpose; no one who en-
gages heartily in that game ever knows why. Ask a great
money-maker what he wants to do with his money—he never
knows. He doesn't make it to do anything with it. He gets
it only that he *may* get it. 'What will you make of what
you have got?' you ask. 'Well, I'll get more,' he says.
Just as, at cricket, you get more runs. There's no use in
the runs, but to get more of them than other people is
the game. And there's no use in the money, but to have
more of it than other people is the game. So all that great
foul city of London there,—rattling, growling, smoking,
stinking,—a ghastly heap of fermenting brickwork, pouring
out poison at every pore,—you fancy it is a city of work?
Not a street of it! It is a great city of play; very
nasty play, and very hard play, but still play. It is only
Lord's cricket ground without the turf,—a huge billiard table
without the cloth, and with pockets as deep as the bottomless
pit; but mainly a billiard table, after all.

1*

Well, the first great English game is this playing at coun-
ters.   It differs from the rest in that it appears always to be
producing money, while every other game is expensive.   But
it does not always produce money.   There's a great difference between 'winning' money and 'making' it; a great
difference between getting it out of another man's pocket
into ours, or filling both.   Collecting money is by no means
the same thing as making it; the tax-gatherer's house is
not the Mint; and much of the apparent gain (so called),
in commerce, is only a form of taxation on carriage or
exchange.

Our next great English game, however, hunting and shooting, is costly altogether; and how much we are fined for it
annually in land, horses, gamekeepers, and game laws, and all
else that accompanies that beautiful and special English
game, I will not endeavour to count now: but note only that,
except for exercise, this is not merely a useless game, but a
deadly one, to all connected with it.   For through horse-
racing, you get every form of what the higher classes everywhere call 'Play,' in distinction from all other plays; that
is—gambling; by no means a beneficial or recreative game:
and, through game-preserving, you get also some curious laying out of ground; that beautiful arrangement of dwelling-
house for man and beast, by which we have grouse and black-
cock—so many brace to the acre, and men and women—so

many brace to the garret. I often wonder what the angelic builders and surveyors—the angelic builders who build the 'many mansions' up above there; and the angelic surveyors, who measured that four-square city with their measuring reeds—I wonder what they think, or are supposed to think, of the laying out of ground by this nation, which has set itself, as it seems, literally to accomplish, word for word, or rather fact for word, in the persons of those poor whom its Master left to represent him, what that Master said of himself—that foxes and birds had homes, but He none.

Then, next to the gentlemen's game of hunting, we must put the ladies' game of dressing. It is not the cheapest of games. I saw a brooch at a jeweller's in Bond Street a fortnight ago, not an inch wide, and without any singular jewel in it, yet worth 3,000*l*. And I wish I could tell you what this 'play' costs, altogether, in England, France, and Russia annually. But it is a pretty game, and on certain terms, I like it; nay, I don't see it played quite as much as I would fain have it. You ladies like to lead the fashion:—by all means lead it—lead it thoroughly, lead it far enough. Dress yourselves nicely, and dress everybody else nicely. Lead the *fashions for the poor* first; make *them* look well, and you yourselves will look, in ways of which you have now no conception, all the better. The fashions you have set for some time among your peasantry are not pretty ones; their doublets are too irregu'arly slashed, and the wind blows too frankly through them.

Then there are other games, wild enough, as I could show you if I had time.

There's playing at literature, and playing at art—very different, both, from working at literature, or working at art, but I've no time to speak of these. I pass to the greatest of all—the play of plays, the great gentlemen's game, which ladies like them best to play at,—the game of War. It is entrancingly pleasant to the imagination; the facts of it, not always so pleasant. We dress for it, however, more finely than for any other sport; and go out to it, not merely in scarlet, as to hunt, but in scarlet and gold, and all manner of fine colours: of course we could fight better in grey, and without feathers; but all nations have agreed that it is good to be well dressed at this play. Then the bats and balls are very costly; our English and French bats, with the balls and wickets, even those which we don't make any use of, costing, I suppose, now about fifteen millions of money annually to each nation; all of which you know is paid for by hard labourer's work in the furrow and furnace. A costly game!—not to speak of its consequences; I will say at present nothing of these. The mere immediate cost of all these plays is what I want you to consider; they all cost deadly work somewhere, as many of us know too well. The jewel-cutter, whose sight fails over the diamonds; the weaver, whose arm fails over the web; the iron-forger, whose breath fails before the furnace—*they* know what work is—they, who have all the work, and none of the play, except a kind they have named for themselves down in the black north country, where 'play' means being laid up by sickness. It is a pretty example for philologists, of varying dialect, this change in the sense of the word 'play,' as used in the black country of Birmingham, and the red and black country of Baden Baden. Yes, gentlemen, and gentlewomen, of England, who think 'one moment unamused a misery, not made for feeble man,' this is what you have brought the word 'play' to mean, in the heart of merry England! You may have your fluting and piping; but there are sad children sitting in the market-place, who indeed cannot say to you, 'We have piped unto you, and ye have not danced:' but eternally shall say to you, 'We have mourned unto you, and ye have not lamented.'

This, then, is the first distinction between the 'upper and lower' classes. And this is one which is by no means necessary; which indeed must, in process of good time, be by all honest men's consent abolished. Men will be taught that an existence of play, sustained by the blood of other creatures, is a good existence for gnats and sucking fish; but not for men: that neither days, nor lives, can be made holy by doing nothing in them: that the best prayer at the beginning of a

day is that we may not lose its moments ; and the best grace
before meat, the consciousness that we have justly earned our
dinner.   And when we have this much of plain Christianity
preached to us again, and enough respect what we regard as
inspiration, as not to think that 'Son, go work to-day in my
vineyard,' means ' Fool, go play to-day in my vineyard,' we
shall all be workers, in one way or another; and this much at
least of the distinction between ' upper ' and 'lower' forgotten·

II. I pass then to our second distinction; between the
rich and poor, between Dives and Lazarus,—distinction
which exists more sternly, I suppose, in this day, than ever
in the world, Pagan or Christian, till now.   I will put it
sharply before you, to begin with, merely by reading two
paragraphs which I cut from two papers that lay on my
breakfast table on the same morning, the 25th of November,
1864.   The piece about the rich Russian at Paris is common-
place enough, and stupid besides (for fifteen francs,—
12s. 6d.,—is nothing for a rich man to give for a couple of
peaches, out of season).   Still, the two paragraphs printed
on the same day are worth putting side by side.

'Such a man is now here.   He is a Russian, and, with
your permission, we will call him Count Teufelskine.   In
dress he is sublime; art is considered in that toilet, the harmony of colour respected, the *chiar' oscuro* evident in well-
selected contrast.   In manners he is dignified—nay, perhaps

apathetic; nothing disturbs the placid serenity of that calm exterior. One day our friend breakfasted *chez* Bignon. When the bill came he read, "Two peaches, 15f." He paid. "Peaches scarce, I presume?" was his sole remark. "No, sir," replied the waiter, "but Teufelskines are." ' *Telegraph*, November 25, 1864.

'Yesterday morning, at eight o'clock, a woman, passing a dung heap in the stone yard near the recently-erected almshouses in Shadwell Gap, High Street, Shadwell, called the attention of a Thames police-constable to a man in a sitting position on the dung heap, and said she was afraid he was dead. Her fears proved to be true. The wretched creature appeared to have been dead several hours. He had perished of cold and wet, and the rain had been beating down on him all night. The deceased was a bone-picker. He was in the lowest stage of poverty, poorly clad, and half-starved. The police had frequently driven him away from the stone yard, between sunset and sunrise, and told him to go home. He selected a most desolate spot for his wretched death. A penny and some bones were found in his pockets. The deceased was between fifty and sixty years of age. Inspector Roberts, of the K division, has given directions for inquiries to be made at the lodging-houses respecting the deceased, to ascertain his identity if possible.'— *Morning Post*, November 25, 1864.

You have the separation thus in brief compass; and I want you to take notice of the 'a penny and some bones were found in his pockets,' and to compare it with this third statement, from the *Telegraph* of January 16th of this year :—

'Again, the dietary scale for adult and juvenile paupers was drawn up by the most conspicuous political economists in England. It is low in quantity, but it is sufficient to support nature; yet within ten years of the passing of the Poor Law Act, we heard of the paupers in the Andover Union gnawing the scraps of putrid flesh and sucking the marrow from the bones of horses which they were employed to crush.'

You see my reason for thinking that our Lazarus of Christianity has some advantage over the Jewish one. Jewish Lazarus expected, or at least prayed, to be fed with crumbs from the rich man's table; but our Lazarus is fed with crumbs from the dog's table.

Now this distinction between rich and poor rests on two bases. Within its proper limits, on a basis which is lawful and everlastingly necessary; beyond them, on a basis unlawful, and everlastingly corrupting the frame-work of society. The lawful basis of wealth is, that a man who works should be paid the fair value of his work; and that if he does not choose to spend it to-day, he should have free leave to keep it, and spend it to-morrow. Thus, an industrious man working

daily, and laying by daily, attains at last the possession of an
accumulated sum of wealth, to which he has absolute right.
The idle person who will not work, and the wasteful person
who lays nothing by, at the end of the same time will be dou-
bly poor—poor in possession, and dissolute in moral habit;
and he will then naturally covet the money which the other
has saved. And if he is then allowed to attack the other,
and rob him of his well-earned wealth, there is no more
any motive for saving, or any reward for good conduct;
and all society is thereupon dissolved, or exists only in sys-
tems of rapine. Therefore the first necessity of social life
is the clearness of national conscience in enforcing the
law—that he should keep who has JUSTLY EARNED.

That law, I say, is the proper basis of distinction between
rich and poor. But there is also a false basis of distinction ; namely, the power held over those who earn wealth
by those who levy or exact it. There will be always a number of men who would fain set themselves to the accumulation of wealth as the sole object of their lives. Necessarily, that class of men is an uneducated class, inferior in
intellect, and more or less cowardly. It is physically
impossible for a well-educated, intellectual, or brave man
to make money the chief object of his thoughts; as physically impossible as it is for him to make his dinner the
principal object of them. All healthy people like their

dinners, but their dinner is not the main object of their
lives. So all healthily minded people like making money—
ought to like it, and to enjoy the sensation of winning it;
but the main object of their life is not money; it is something better than money. A good soldier, for instance,
mainly wishes to do his fighting well. He is glad of his
pay—very properly so, and justly grumbles when you
keep him ten years without it—still, his main notion of life
is to win battles, not to be paid for winning them. So
of clergymen. They like pew-rents, and baptismal fees,
of course; but yet, if they are brave and well educated,
the pew-rent is not the sole object of their lives, and the
baptismal fee is not the sole purpose of the baptism; the
clergyman's object is essentially to baptize and preach, not
to be paid for preaching. So of doctors. They like fees
no doubt,—ought to like them; yet if they are brave and
well educated, the entire object of their lives is not fees.
They, on the whole, desire to cure the sick; and,—if they
are good doctors, and the choice were fairly put to
them,—would rather cure their patient, and lose their fee,
than kill him, and get it. And so with all other brave and
rightly trained men; their work is first, their fee second—
very important always, but still *second*. But in every
nation, as I said, there are a vast class who are ill-edu-
cated, cowardly, and more or less stupid. And with these

people, just as certainly the fee is first, and the work
second, as with brave people the work is first and the fee
second. And this is no small distinction. It is the whole
distinction in a man; distinction between life and death *in*
him, between heaven and hell *for* him. You cannot serve
two masters;—you *must* serve one or other. If your work
is first with you, and your fee second, work is your master,
and the lord of work, who is God. But if your fee is
first with you, and your work second, fee is your master,
and the lord of fee, who is the Devil; and not only the
Devil, but the lowest of devils—the 'least erected fiend
that fell.' So there you have it in brief terms; Work
first—you are God's servants; Fee first—you are the
Fiend's. And it makes a difference, now and ever, believe
me, whether you serve Him who has on His vesture and
thigh written, 'King of Kings,' and whose service is perfect freedom; or him on whose vesture and thigh the
name is written, 'Slave of Slaves,' and whose service is
perfect slavery.

However, in every nation there are, and must always be
a certain number of these Fiend's servants, who have it
principally for the object of their lives to make money.
They are always, as I said, more or less stupid, and can
not conceive of anything else so nice as money. Stupidity
is always the basis of the Judas bargain. We do great

injustice to Iscariot, in thinking him wicked above all common wickedness. He was only a common money-lover,
and, like all money-lovers, didn't understand Christ ;—
couldn't make out the worth of Him, or meaning of Him.
He didn't want Him to be killed. He was horror-struck
when he found that Christ would be killed; threw his
money away instantly, and hanged himself. How many of
our present money-seekers, think you, would have the grace
to hang themselves, whoever was killed? But Judas was
a common, selfish, muddle-headed, pilfering fellow; his
hand always in the bag of the poor, not caring for them
He didn't understand Christ;—yet believed in Him, much
more than most of us do; had seen Him do miracles,
thought He was quite strong enough to shift for Himself,
and he, Judas, might as well make his own little bye-per-
quisites out of the affair. Christ would come out of it
well enough, and he have his thirty pieces. Now, that is
the money-seeker's idea, all over the world. He doesn't
hate Christ, but can't understand Him—doesn't care for
Him—sees no good in that benevolent business; makes his
own little job out of it at all events, come what will. And
thus, out of every mass of men, you have a certain number of bag-men—your 'fee-first' men, whose main object is
to make money. And they do make it—make it in all
sorts of unfair ways, chiefly by the weight and force of

money itself, or what is called the power of capital; that is to say, the power which money, once obtained, has over the labour of the poor, so that the capitalist can take all its produce to himself, except the labourer's food. That is the modern Judas's way of 'carrying the bag,' and 'bearing what is put therein.'

Nay, but (it is asked) how is that an unfair advantage? Has not the man who has worked for the money a right to use it as he best can? No; in this respect, money is now exactly what mountain promontories over public roads were in old times. The barons fought for them fairly :—the strongest and cunningest got them; then fortified them, and made everyone who passed below pay toll. Well, capital now is exactly what crags were then. Men fight fairly (we will, at least, grant so much, though it is more than we ought) for their money; but, once having got it, the fortified millionaire can make everybody who passes below pay toll to his million, and build another tower of his money castle. And I can tell you, the poor vagrants by the roadside suffer now quite as much from the bag-baron, as ever they did from the crag-baron. Bags and crags have just the same result on rags. I have not time, however, to-night to show you in how many ways the power of capital is unjust; but this one great principle I have to assert—you will find it quite indisputably true —that whenever money is the principal object of life with

either man or nation, it is both got ill, and spent ill; and does
harm both in the getting and spending; but when it is not
the principal object, it and all other things will be well got,
and well spent. And here is the test, with every man, of
whether money is the principal object with him, or not. If
in mid-life he could pause and say, " Now I have enough to
live upon, I'll live upon it; and having well earned it, I will
also well spend it, and go out of the world poor, as I came
into it," then money is not principal with him; but if, having
enough to live upon in the manner befitting his character and
rank, he still wants to make more, and to *die* rich, then money
is the principal object with him, and it becomes a curse to
himself, and generally to those who spend it after him. For
you know it *must* be spent some day; the only question is
whether the man who makes it shall spend it, or some one
else. And generally it is better for the maker to spend it,
for he will know best its value and use. This is the true law
of life. And if a man does not choose thus to spend his
money, he must either hoard it or lend it, and the worst thing
he can generally do is to lend it; for borrowers are nearly
always ill-spenders, and it is with lent money that all evil is
mainly done, and all unjust war protracted.

For observe what the real fact is, respecting loans to foreign military governments, and how strange it is. If your
little boy came to you to ask for money to spend in squibs

and crackers, you would think twice before you gave it him ; and you would have some idea that it was wasted, when you saw it fly off in fireworks, even though he did no mischief with it. But the Russian children, and Austrian children, come to you, borrowing money, not to spend in innocent squibs, but in cartridges and bayonets to attack you in India with, and to keep down all noble life in Italy with, and to murder Polish women and children with; and *that* you will give at once, because they pay you interest for it. Now, in order to pay you that interest, they must tax every working peasant in their dominions; and on that work you live. You therefore at once rob the Austrian peasant, assassinate or banish the Polish peasant, and you live on the produce of the theft, and the bribe for the assassination ! That is the broad fact—that is the practical meaning of your foreign loans, and of most large interest of money ; and then you quarrel with Bishop Colenso, forsooth, as if *he* denied the Bible, and you believed it ! though, wretches as you are, every deliberate act of your lives is a new defiance of its primary orders ; and as if, for most of the rich men of England at this moment, it were not indeed to be desired, as the best thing at least for *them*, that the Bible should *not* be true, since against them these words are written in it : 'The rust of your gold and silver shall be a witness against you, and shall eat your flesh, as it were fire.'

III. I pass now to our third condition of separation, between the men who work with the hand, and those who work
with the head.

And here we have at last an inevitable distinction.   There
must be work done by the arms, or none of us could live.
There *must* be work done by the brains, or the life we get
would not be worth having.   And the same men cannot do
both.   There is rough work to be done, and rough men must
do it; there is gentle work to be done, and gentlemen
must do it; and it is physically impossible that one class should
do, or divide, the work of the other.   And it is of no use to
try to conceal this sorrowful fact by fine words, and to talk
to the workman about the honourableness of manual labour,
and the dignity of humanity.   That is a grand old proverb
of Sancho Panza's, 'Fine words butter no parsnips;' and I
can tell you that, all over England just now, you workmen
are buying a great deal too much butter at that dairy.   Rough
work, honourable or not, takes the life out of us; and the man
who has been heaving clay out of a ditch all day, or driving
an express train against the north wind all night, or holding
a collier's helm in a gale on a lee-shore, or whirling white hot
iron at a furnace mouth, that man is not the same at the end
of his day, or night, as one who has been sitting in a quiet
room, with everything comfortable about him, reading books,
or classing butterflies, or painting pictures.   If it is any com-

fort to you to be told that the rough work is the more honourable of the two, I should be sorry to take that much of consolation from you; and in some sense I need not. The rough work is at all events real, honest, and, generally, though not always, useful; while the fine work is, a great deal of it, foolish and false as well as fine, and therefore dishonourable : but when both kinds are equally well and worthily done, the head's is the noble work, and the hand's the ignoble ; and of all hand work whatsoever, necessary for the maintenance of life, those old words, 'In the sweat of thy face thou shalt eat bread,' indicate that the inherent nature of it is one of calamity ; and that the ground, cursed for our sake, casts also some shadow of degradation into our contest with its thorn and its thistle ; so that all nations have held their days honourable, or 'holy,' and constituted them 'holydays' or 'holidays,' by making them days of rest ; and the promise, which, among all our distant hopes, seems to cast the chief brightness over death, is that blessing of the dead who die in the Lord, that 'they rest from their labours, and their works do follow them.'

And thus the perpetual question and contest must arise, who is to do this rough work? and how is the worker of it to be comforted, redeemed, and rewarded ? and what kind of play should he have, and what rest, in this world, sometimes, as well as in the next ? Well, my good working friends, these questions will take a little time to answer yet. They must be answered: all good men are occupied with them, and all honest thinkers. There's grand head work doing about them; but much must be discovered, and much attempted in vain, before anything decisive can be told you. Only note these few particulars, which are already sure.

As to the distribution of the hard work. None of us, or very few of us, do either hard or soft work because we think we ought; but because we have chanced to fall into the way of it, and cannot help ourselves. Now, nobody does anything well that they cannot help doing: work is only done well when it is done with a will; and no man has a thoroughly sound will unless he knows he is doing what he should, and is in his place. And, depend upon it, all work must be done at last, not in a disorderly, scrambling, doggish way, but in an ordered, soldierly, human way—a lawful way. Men are enlisted for the labour that kills—the labour of war: they are counted, trained, fed, dressed, and praised for that. Let them be enlisted also for the labour that feeds: let them be counted, trained, fed, dressed, praised for that. Teach the plough exercise as carefully as you do the sword exercise, and let the officers of troops of life be held as much gentlemen as the officers of troops of death ; and all is done: but neither this, nor any other right thing, can be accomplished—you can't even see your way to it—unless, first of all, both servant and master are resolved that, come what will of it, they will do each other justice. People are perpetually squabbling about what will be best to do, or easiest to do, or adviseablest to do, or profitablest to do ; but they never, so far as I hear them talk, ever ask what it is *just* to do. And it is the law of heaven that you shall not be able to judge what is wise or easy, unless you are first resolved to judge what is just, and to do it. That is the one thing constantly reiterated by our Master—the order of all others that is given oftenest—'Do justice and judgment.' That's your Bible order; that's the 'Service of God,' not praying nor psalm-singing. You are told, indeed, to sing psalms when you are merry, and to pray when you need anything ; and, by the perversion of the Evil Spirit, we get to think that praying and psalm-singing are 'service.' If a child finds itself in want of anything, it runs in and asks its father for it —does it call that, doing its father a service ? If it begs for a toy or a piece of cake—does it call that serving its father ? That, with God, is prayer, and He likes to hear it : He likes you to ask Him for cake when you want it ; but He does n't call that 'serving Him.' Begging is not serving : God likes mere beggars as little as you do—He likes honest servants, not beggars. So when a child loves its father very much, and is very happy, it may sing little songs about him ; but it does n't call that serving its father; neither is singing songs about God, serving God. It is enjoying ourselves, if it's anything; most probably it is nothing; but if it's anything, it is serving ourselves, not God. And yet we are impudent enough to call our beggings and chauntings 'Divine Service:' we say 'Divine service will be "performed"' (that's our word—the form of it gone through) 'at eleven o'clock.' Alas!—unless we perform Divine service in every willing act of our life, we never perform it at all. The one Divine work—the one ordered sacrifice—is to do justice; and it is the last we are ever inclined to do. Anything rather than that! As much charity as you choose, but no justice. 'Nay,' you will say, 'charity is greater than justice.' Yes, it is greater; it is the summit of justice—it is the temple of which justice is the foundation. But you can't have the top without the bottom; you cannot build upon charity. You must build upon justice, for this main reason, that you have not, at first, charity to build with. It is the last reward of good work. Do justice to your brother (you can do that, whether you love him or not), and you will come to love him. But do injustice to him, because you don't love him; and you will come to hate him. It is all very fine to think you can build upon charity to begin with; but you will find all you have got to begin with, begins at home, and is essentially love of yourself. You well-to-do people, for instance, who

are here to-night, will go to 'Divine service' next Sunday,
all nice and tidy, and your little children will have their tight
little Sunday boots on, and lovely little Sunday feathers in
their hats; and you'll think, complacently and piously, how
lovely they look! So they do: and you love them heartily,
and you like sticking feathers in their hats. That's all right:
that *is* charity; but it is charity beginning at home. Then
you will come to the poor little crossing-sweeper, got up
also,—it, in its Sunday dress,—the dirtiest rags it has,—that
it may beg the better: we shall give it a penny, and think
how good we are. That's charity going abroad. But what
does Justice say, walking and watching near us? Christian
Justice has been strangely mute, and seemingly blind; and,
if not blind, decrepit, this many a day: she keeps her accounts still, however—quite steadily—doing them at nights,
carefully, with her bandage off, and through acutest specta-
cles (the only modern scientific invention she cares about).
You must put your ear down ever so close to her lips to hear
her speak; and then you will start at what she first whispers,
for it will certainly be, 'Why shouldn't that little crossing-
sweeper have a feather on its head, as well as your own
child?' Then you may ask Justice, in an amazed manner,
'How she can possibly be so foolish as to think children
could sweep crossings with feathers on their heads?' Then
you stoop again, and Justice says—still in her dull, stupid

way—' Then, why don't you, every other Sunday, leave your child to sweep the crossing, and take the little sweeper to church in a hat and feather?' Mercy on us (you think), what will she say next? And you answer, of course, that ' you don't, because every body ought to remain content in the position in which Providence has placed them.' Ah, my friends, that's the gist of the whole question. *Did* Providence put them in that position, or did *you?* You knock a man into a ditch, and then you tell him to remain content in the 'position in which Providence has placed him.' That's modern Christianity. You say—' *We* did not knock him into the ditch.' How do you know what you have done, or are doing? That's just what we have all got to know, and what we shall never know, until the question with us every morning, is, not how to do the gainful thing, but how to do the just thing; nor until we are at least so far on the way to being Christian, as to have understood that maxim of the poor half-way Mahometan, 'One hour in the execution of justice is worth seventy years of prayer.'

Supposing, then, we have it determined with appropriate justice, *who* is to do the hand work, the next questions must be how the hand-workers are to be paid, and how they are to be refreshed, and what play they are to have. Now, the possible quantity of play depends on the possible quantity of pay; and the quantity of pay is not a matter for consideration to hand-workers only, but to all workers. Generally, good, useful work, whether of the hand or head, is either ill-paid, or not paid at all. I don't say it should be so, but it always is so. People, as a rule, only pay for being amused or being cheated, not for being served. Five thousand a year to your talker, and a shilling a day to your fighter, digger, and thinker, is the rule. None of the best head work in art, literature, or science, is ever paid for. How much do you think Homer got for his Iliad? or Dante for his Paradise? only bitter bread and salt, and going up and down other people's stairs. In science, the man who discovered the telescope, and first saw heaven, was paid with a dungeon; the man who invented the microscope, and first saw earth, died of starvation, driven from his home: it is indeed very clear that God means all thoroughly good work and talk to be done for nothing. Baruch, the scribe, did not get a penny a line for writing Jeremiah's second roll for him, I fancy; and St. Stephen did not get bishop's pay for that long sermon of his to the Pharisees; nothing but stones. For indeed that is the world-father's proper payment. So surely as any of the world's children work for the world's good, honestly, with head and heart; and come to it, saying, ' Give us a little bread, just to keep the life in us,' the world-father answers them, ' No, my children, not bread; a stone, if you like, or as many as you need, to keep you quiet.' But the hand-workers are not so ill off as all this comes to. The worst that can happen to *you* is to break stones; not be broken by them. And for you there will come a time for better payment; some day, assuredly, more pence will be paid to Peter the Fisherman, and fewer to Peter the Pope; we shall pay people not quite so much for talking in Parliament and doing nothing, as for holding their tongues out of it and doing something; we shall pay our ploughman a little more and our lawyer a little less, and so on: but, at least, we may even now take care that whatever work is done shall be fully paid for; and the man who does it paid for it, not somebody else; and that it shall be done in an orderly, soldierly, well-guided, wholesome way, under good captains and lieutenants of labour; and that it shall have its appointed times of rest, and enough of them; and that in those times the play shall be wholesome play, not in theatrical gardens, with tin flowers and gas sunshine, and girls dancing because of their misery; but in true gardens, with real flowers, and real sunshine, and children dancing because of their gladness; so that truly the streets shall be full (the 'streets,' mind you, not the gutters) of children, playing in the midst thereof. We may take care that working-men shall have at least as good books to read as anybody else, when they've time to read them; and as comfortable firesides to sit at as anybody else, when they've time to sit at them.

This, I think, can be managed for you, my working friends, in the good time.

IV. I must go on, however, to our last head, concerning ourselves all, as workers. What is wise work, and what is foolish work? What the difference between sense and non sense, in daily occupation?

Well, wise work is, briefly, work *with* God. Foolish work is work *against* God. And work done with God, which He will help, may be briefly described as 'Putting in Order'—that is, enforcing God's law of order, spiritual and material, over men and things. The first thing you have to do, essentially; the real 'good work' is, with respect to men, to enforce justice, and with respect to things, to enforce tidiness, and fruitfulness. And against these two great human deeds, justice and order, there are perpetually two great demons contending,—the devil of iniquity, or inequity, and the devil of disorder, or of death; for death is only consummation of disorder. You have to fight these two fiends daily. So far as you don't fight against the fiend of iniquity, you work for him. You 'work iniquity,' and the judgment upon you, for all your 'Lord, Lord's,' will be 'Depart from me, ye that work iniquity.' And so far as you do not resist the fiend of disorder, you work disorder, and you yourself do the work of Death, which is sin, and has for its wages, Death himself.

2*

Observe then, all wise work is mainly threefold in charac
ter. It is honest, useful, and cheerful.

I. It is HONEST. I hardly know anything more strange
than that you recognise honesty in play, and you do not in
work. In your lightest games, you have always some one
to see what you call 'fair-play.' In boxing, you must hit
fair; in racing, start fair. Your English watchword is fair-
play, your English hatred, foul-play. Did it ever strike you
that you wanted another watchword also, fair-work, and
another hatred also, foul-work? Your prize-fighter has
some honour in him yet; and so have the men in the ring
round him: they will judge him to lose the match, by foul
hitting. But your prize-merchant gains his match by foul
selling, and no one cries out against that. You drive a
gambler out of the gambling-room who loads dice, but you
leave a tradesman in flourishing business, who loads scales!
For observe, all dishonest dealing *is* loading scales. What
does it matter whether I get short weight, adulterate substance, or dishonest fabric? The fault in the fabric is incom-
parably the worst of the two. Give me short measure of
food, and I only lose by you; but give me adulterate food,
and I die by you. Here, then, is your chief duty, you workmen and tradesmen—to be true to yourselves, and to us who
would help you. We can do nothing for you, nor you for
yourselves, without honesty. Get that, you get all; with-

out that, your suffrages, your reforms, your free-trade mea-
sures, your institutions of science, are all in vain. It is useless to put your heads together, if you can't put your hearts
together. Shoulder to shoulder, right hand to right hand,
among yourselves, and no wrong hand to anybody else, and
you'll win the world yet.

II. Then, secondly, wise work is USEFUL. No man minds,
or ought to mind, its being hard, if only it comes to something; but when it is hard, and comes to nothing; when all
our bees' business turns to spiders'; and for honey-comb we
have only resultant cobweb, blown away by the next breeze
—that is the cruel thing for the worker. Yet do we ever
ask ourselves, personally, or even nationally, whether our
work is coming to anything or not? We don't care to keep
what has been nobly done; still less do we care to do nobly
what others would keep; and, least of all, to make the work
itself useful instead of deadly to the doer, so as to use his
life indeed, but not to waste it. Of all wastes, the greatest
waste that you can commit is the waste of labour. If you
went down in the morning into your dairy, and you found
that your youngest child had got down before you; and
that he and the cat were at play together, and that he had
poured out all the cream on the floor for the cat to lap up,
you would scold the child, and be sorry the milk was wasted.
But if, instead of wooden bowls with milk in them, there

are golden bowls with human life in them, and instead of
the cat to play with—the devil to play with; and you yourself the player; and instead of leaving that golden bowl to
be broken by God at the fountain, you break it in the dust
yourself, and pour the human blood out on the ground for
the fiend to lick up—that is no waste! What! you perhaps
think, 'to waste the labour of men is not to kill them.' Is it
not? I should like to know how you could kill them more
utterly—kill them with second deaths, seventh deaths, hun-
dredfold deaths? It is the slightest way of killing to stop
a man's breath. Nay, the hunger, and the cold, and the
little whistling bullets—our love-messengers between nation
and nation—have brought pleasant messages from us to
many a man before now; orders of sweet release, and leave
at last to go where he will be most welcome and most
happy. At the worst you do but shorten his life, you do
not corrupt his life. But if you put him to base labour, if
you bind his thoughts, if you blind his eyes, if you blunt his
hopes, if you steal his joys, if you stunt his body, and blast
his soul, and at last leave him not so much as to reap the
poor fruit of his degradation, but gather that for yourself,
and dismiss him to the grave, when you have done with him,
having, so far as in you lay, made the walls of that grave
everlasting (though, indeed, I fancy the goodly bricks of
some of our family vaults will hold closer in the resurrection

day than the sod over the labourer's head), this you think is
no waste, and no sin!

III. Then, lastly, wise work is CHEERFUL, as a child's work
is. And now I want you to take one thought home with
you, and let it stay with you.

Everybody in this room has been taught to pray daily,
'Thy kingdom come.' Now, if we hear a man swear in the
streets, we think it very wrong, and say he 'takes God's
name in vain.' But there's a twenty times worse way of
taking His name in vain, than that. It is to *ask God for
what we don't want.* He does n't like that sort of prayer. If
you don't want a thing, don't ask for it: such asking is the
worst mockery of your King you can mock Him with; the
soldiers striking Him on the head with the reed was nothing
to that. If you do not wish for His kingdom, don't pray for
it. But if you do, you must do more than pray for it; you
must work for it. And, to work for it, you must know what
it is: we have all prayed for it many a day without thinking.
Observe, it is a kingdom that is to come to us; we are not
to go to it. Also, it is not to be a kingdom of the dead, but
of the living. Also, it is not to come all at once, but quietly;
nobody knows how. 'The kingdom of God cometh not with
observation.' Also, it is not to come outside of us, but in
the hearts of us: 'the kingdom of God is within you.' And,
being within us, it is not a thing to be seen, but to be felt;

and though it brings all substance of good with it, it does
not consist in that: 'the kingdom of God is not meat and
drink, but righteousness, peace, and joy in the Holy Ghost:'
joy, that is to say, in the holy, healthful, and helpful Spirit.
Now, if we want to work for this kingdom, and to bring
it, and enter into it, there's just one condition to be first
accepted. You must enter it as children, or not at all;
'Whosoever will not receive it as a little child shall not enter
therein.' And again, 'Suffer little children to come unto
me, and forbid them not, for of such is the kingdom of
heaven.'

Of such, observe. Not of children themselves, but of such
as children. I believe most mothers who read that text
think that all heaven is to be full of babies. But that's not
so. There will be children there, but the hoary head is the
crown. 'Length of days, and long life and peace,' that is
the blessing, not to die in babyhood. Children die but for
their parents' sins ; God means them to live, but He can't let
them always ; then they have their earlier place in heaven :
and the little child of David, vainly prayed for;—the little
child of Jeroboam, killed by its mother's step on its own
threshold,—they will be there. But weary old David, and
weary old Barzillai, having learned children's lessons at last,
will be there too . and the one question for us all, young or
old, is, have we learned our child's lesson ? it is the *character* of

children we want, and must gain at our peril; let us see, briefly, in what it consists.

The first character of right childhood is that it is Modest A well-bred child does not think it can teach its parents, or that it knows everything. It may think its father and mother know everything,—perhaps that all grown-up people know everything; very certainly it is sure that *it* does not. And it is always asking questions, and wanting to know more. Well, that is the first character of a good and wise man at his work. To know that he knows very little;—to perceive that there are many above him wiser than he ; and to be always asking questions, wanting to learn, not to teach. No one ever teaches well who wants to teach, or governs well who wants to govern ; it is an old saying (Plato's, but I know not if his, first), and as wise as old.

Then, the second character of right childhood is to be Faithful. Perceiving that its father knows best what is good for it, and having found always, when it has tried its own way against his, that he was right and it was wrong, a noble child trusts him at last wholly, gives him its hand, and will walk blindfold with him, if he bids it. And that is the true character of all good men also, as obedient workers, or sol-diers under captains. They must trust their captains ;—they are bound for their lives to choose none but those whom they *can* trust. Then, they are not always to be thinking that what seems strange to them, or wrong in what they are desired to do, *is* strange or wrong. They know their captain : where he leads they must follow, what he bids, they must do ; and without this trust and faith, without this captainship and soldiership, no great deed, no great salvation, is possible to man. Among all the nations it is only when this faith is attained by them that they become great: the Jew, the Greek, and the Mahometan, agree at least in testifying to this. It was a deed of this absolute trust which made Abraham the father of the faithful ; it was the declaration of the power of God as captain over all men, and the acceptance of a leader appointed by Him as commander of the faithful, which laid the foundation of whatever national power yet exists in the East; and the deed of the Greeks, which has become the type of unselfish and noble soldiership to all lands, and to all times, was commemorated, on the tomb of those who gave their lives to do it, in the most pathetic, so far as I know, or can feel, of all human utterances: ' Oh, stranger, go and tell our people that we are lying here, having *obeyed* their words.'

Then the third character of right childhood is to be Loving and Generous. Give a little love to a child, and you get a great deal back. It loves everything near it, when it is a right kind of child—would hurt nothing, would give the best it has away, always, if you need it—does not lay plans for getting everything in the house for itself, and delights in helping people ; you cannot please it so much as by giving it a chance of being useful, in ever so little a way. ⸗

And because of all these characters, lastly, it is Cheerful. Putting its trust in its father, it is careful for nothing—being full of love to every creature, it is happy always, whether in its play or in its duty. Well, that's the great worker's character also. Taking no thought for the morrow; taking thought only for the duty of the day ; trusting somebody else to take care of to-morrow ; knowing indeed what labour is, but not what sorrow is; and always ready for play—beautiful play,—for lovely human play is like the play of the Sun. There's a worker for you. He, steady to his time, is set as a strong man to run his course, but also, he *rejoiceth* as a strong man to run his course. See how he plays in the morning, with the mists below, and the clouds above, with a ray here and a flash there, and a shower of jewels everywhere ;—that's the Sun's play; and great human play is like his—all various —all full of light and life, and tender, as the dew of the morning.

So then, you have the child's character in these four things— Humility, Faith, Charity, and Cheerfulness. That's what you have got to be converted to. ' Except ye be converted and become as little children '—You hear much of conversion now-a-days ; but people always seem to think they have got to be

made wretched by conversion,—to be converted to long
faces.   No, friends, you have got to be converted to short
ones; you have to repent into childhood, to repent into
delight, and delightsomeness.   You can't go into a con-
venticle but you'll hear plenty of talk of backsliding.
Backsliding, indeed! I can tell you, on the ways most
of us go, the faster we slide back the better.   Slide back
into the cradle, if going on is into the grave—back, I
tell you; back—out of your long faces, and into your
long clothes.   It is among children only, and as children
only, that you will find medicine for your healing and
true wisdom for your teaching.   There is poison in the
counsels of the *men* of this world; the words they speak
are all bitterness, 'the poison of asps is under their lips,'
but, 'the sucking child shall play by the hole of the
asp.'   There is death in the looks of men.   'Their eyes
are privily set against the poor;' they are as the uncharm-
able serpent, the cockatrice, which slew by seeing.   But
'the weaned child shall lay his hand on the cockatrice
den.'   There is death in the steps of men: 'their feet
are swift to shed blood; they have compassed us in
our steps like the lion that is greedy of his prey, and
the young lion lurking in secret places,' but, in that kingdom, the wolf shall lie down with the lamb, and the
fatling with the lion, and 'a little child shall lead them.'

There is death in the thoughts of men : the world is one wide riddle to them, darker and darker as it draws to a close ; but the secret of it is known to the child and the Lord of heaven and earth is most to be thanked in that 'He has hidden these things from the wise and prudent, and has revealed them unto babes.' Yes, and there is death—infinitude of death in the principalities and powers of men. As far as the east is from the west, so far our sins are—*not* set from us, but multiplied around us : the Sun himself, think you he *now* 'rejoices' to run his course, when he plunges westward to the horizon, so widely red, not with clouds, but blood ? And it will be red more widely yet. Whatever drought of the early and latter rain may be, there will be none of that red rain. You fortify yourselves, you arm yourselves. against it in vain ; the enemy and avenger will be upon you also, unless you learn that it is not out of the mouths of the knitted gun, or the smoothed rifle, but 'out of the mouths of babes and sucklings' that the strength is ordain- ed, which shall 'still the enemy and avenger.'

TRAFFIC.

LECTURE II.

TRAFFIC.

(*Delivered in the Town Hall, Bradford.*)

MY good Yorkshire friends, you asked me down here
among your hills that I might talk to you about this
Exchange you are going to build: but earnestly and seriously
asking you to pardon me, I am going to do nothing of
the kind. I cannot talk, or at least can say very little,
about this same Exchange. I must talk of quite other
things, though not willingly;—I could not deserve your
pardon, if when you invited me to speak on one subject,
I wilfully spoke on another. But I cannot speak, to
purpose, of anything about which I do not care; and most
simply and sorrowfully I have to tell you, in the outset, that
I do *not* care about this Exchange of yours.

If, however, when you sent me your invitation, I had
answered, 'I won't come, I don't care about the Exchange
of Bradford,' you would have been justly offended with
me, not knowing the reasons of so blunt a carelessness.
So I have come down, hoping that you will patiently let
me tell you why, on this, and many other such occasions,

I now remain silent, when formerly I should have caught
at the opportunity of speaking to a gracious audience.

In a word, then, I do not care about this Exchange,—
because *you* don't; and because you know perfectly well
I cannot make you. Look at the essential circumstances
of the case, which you, as business men, know perfectly
well, though perhaps you think I forget them. You are
going to spend 30,000*l*., which to you, collectively, is nothing;
the buying a new coat is, as to the cost of it, a much
more important matter of consideration to me than building
a new Exchange is to you. But you think you may as
well have the right thing for your money. You know
there are a great many odd styles of architecture about;
you don't want to do anything ridiculous; you hear of
me, among others, as a respectable architectural man-milliner:
and you send for me, that I may tell you the leading
fashion; and what is, in our shops, for the moment, the
newest and sweetest thing in pinnacles.

Now, pardon me for telling you frankly, you cannot have
good architecture merely by asking people's advice on occasion. All good architecture is the expression of national life
and character; and it is produced by a prevalent and eager
national taste, or desire for beauty. And I want you to think
a little of the deep significance of this word 'taste;' for no
statement of mine has been more earnestly or oftener contro-

verted than that good taste is essentially a moral quality.
'No,' say many of my antagonists, 'taste is one thing, morality is another. Tell us what is pretty; we shall be glad to
know that; but preach no sermons to us.'

Permit me, therefore, to fortify this old dogma of mine
somewhat. Taste is not only a part and an index of morality—it is the ONLY morality. The first, and last, and closest
trial question to any living creature is, 'What do you like?'
Tell me what you like, and I'll tell you what you are. Go
out into the street, and ask the first man or woman you meet,
what their 'taste' is, and if they answer candidly, you know
them, body and soul. 'You, my friend in the rags, with the
unsteady gait, what do *you* like?' 'A pipe and a quartern
of gin.' I know you. 'You, good woman, with the quick
step and tidy bonnet, what do you like?' 'A swept hearth
and a clean tea-table, and my husband opposite me, and a
baby at my breast.' Good, I know you also. 'You, little
girl with the golden hair and the soft eyes, what do you like?'
'My canary, and a run among the wood hyacinths.' 'You,
little boy with the dirty hands and the low forehead, what do
you like?' 'A shy at the sparrows, and a game at pitch-
farthing.' Good; we know them all now. What more need
we ask?

'Nay,' perhaps you answer: 'we need rather to ask what
these people and children do, than what they like. If they *do*

3

right, it is no matter that they like what is wrong; and if they *do* wrong, it is no matter that they like what is right. Doing is the great thing; and it does not matter that the man likes drinking, so that he does not drink; nor that the little girl likes to be kind to her canary, if she will not learn her lessons; nor that the little boy likes throwing stones at the sparrows, if he goes to the Sunday school.' Indeed, for a short time, and in a provisional sense, this is true. For if, resolutely, people do what is right, in time they come to like doing it. But they only are in a right moral state when they *have* come to like doing it; and as long as they don't like it, they are still in a vicious state. The man is not in health of body who is always thirsting for the bottle in the cupboard, though he bravely bears his thirst; but the man who heartily enjoys water in the morning and wine in the evening, each in its proper quantity and time. And the entire object of true education is to make people not merely *do* the right things, but *enjoy* the right things—not merely industrious, but to love industry—not merely learned, but to love knowledge—not merely pure, but to love purity—not merely just, but to hunger and thirst after justice.

But you may answer or think, 'Is the liking for outside ornaments,—for pictures, or statues, or furniture, or architecture,—a moral quality?' Yes, most surely, if a rightly set liking. Taste for *any* pictures or statues is not a moral quality, but taste for good ones is. Only here again we have to define the word 'good.' I don't mean by 'good,' clever —or learned—or difficult in the doing. Take a picture by Teniers, of sots quarrelling over their dice: it is an entirely clever picture; so clever that nothing in its kind has ever been done equal to it; but it is also an entirely base and evil picture. It is an expression of delight in the prolonged contemplation of a vile thing, and delight in that is an 'unmannered,' or 'immoral' quality. It is 'bad taste' in the profoundest sense—it is the taste of the devils. On the other hand, a picture of Titian's, or a Greek statue, or a Greek coin, or a Turner landscape, expresses delight in the perpetual contemplation of a good and perfect thing. That is an entirely moral quality—it is the taste of the angels. And all delight in art, and all love of it, resolve themselves into simple love of that which deserves love. That deserving is the quality which we call 'loveliness'—(we ought to have an opposite word, hateliness, to be said of the things which deserve to be hated); and it is not an indifferent nor optional thing whether we love this or that; but it is just the vital function of all our being. What we *like* determines what we *are*, and is the sign of what we are; and to teach taste is inevitably to form character. As I was thinking over this, in walking up Fleet Street the other day, my eye caught the title of a book standing open in a bookseller's

window. It was—'On the necessity of the diffusion of taste
among all classes.' 'Ah,' I thought to myself, 'my classify-
ing friend, when you have diffused your taste, where will
your classes be ? The man who likes what you like, belongs
to the same class with you, I think. Inevitably so. You
may put him to other work if you choose; but, by the
condition you have brought him into, he will dislike
the other work as much as you would yourself. You get
hold of a scavenger, or a costermonger, who enjoyed the
Newgate Calendar for literature, and "Pop goes the
Weasel" for music. You think you can make him
like Dante and Beethoven? I wish you joy of your
lessons; but if you do, you have made a gentleman of
him:—he won't like to go back to his costermonger-
ing.'

And so completely and unexceptionally is this so, that, if
I had time to-night, I could show you that a nation cannot be
affected by any vice, or weakness, without expressing it, legibly, and for ever, either in bad art, or by want of art; and
that there is no national virtue, small or great, which is not
manifestly expressed in all the art which circumstances en
able the people possessing that virtue to produce. Take, for
instance, your great English virtue of enduring and patient
courage. You have at present in England only one art of
any consequence—that is, iron-working. You know thoroughly

well how to cast and hammer iron. Now, do you think in
those masses of lava which you build volcanic cones to melt,
and which you forge at the mouths of the Infernos you have
created; do you think, on those iron plates, your courage
and endurance are not written for ever—not merely with an
iron pen, but on iron parchment? And take also your great
English vice—European vice—vice of all the world—vice of all
other worlds that roll or shine in heaven, bearing with them
yet the atmosphere of hell—the vice of jealousy, which
brings competition into your commerce, treachery into your
councils, and dishonour into your wars—that vice which has
rendered for you, and for your next neighbouring nation, the
daily occupations of existence no longer possible, but with
the mail upon your breasts and the sword loose in its sheath;
so that, at last, you have realised for all the multitudes of the
two great peoples who lead the so-called civilisation of the
earth,—you have realised for them all, I say, in person and
in policy, what was once true only of the rough Border
riders of your Cheviot hills—

'They carved at the meal
With gloves of steel,
And they drank the red wine through the helmet barr'd;—

do you think that this national shame and dastardliness of
heart are not written as legibly on every rivet of your iron
armour as the strength of the right hands that forged it?

Friends, I know not whether this thing be the more ludicrous or the more melancholy. It is quite unspeakably both. Suppose, instead of being now sent for by you, I had been sent for by some private gentleman, living in a suburban house, with his garden separated only by a fruit-wall from his next door neighbour's; and he had called me to consult with him on the furnishing of his drawing-room. I begin looking about me, and find the walls rather bare; I think such and such a paper might be desirable—perhaps a little fresco here and there on the ceiling—a damask curtain or so at the windows. 'Ah,' says my employer, 'damask curtains, indeed! That's all very fine, but you know I can't afford that kind of thing just now!' 'Yet the world credits you with a splendid income!' 'Ah, yes,' says my friend, 'but do you know, at present, I am obliged to spend it nearly all in steel-traps?' 'Steel-traps! for whom?' 'Why, for that fellow on the other side the wall, you know: we're very good friends, capital friends; but we are obliged to keep our traps set on both sides of the wall; we could not possibly keep on friendly terms without them, and our spring guns. The worst of it is, we are both clever fellows enough; and there's never a day passes that we don't find out a new trap, or a new gun-barrel, or something; we spend about fifteen millions a year each in our traps, take it all together; and I don't see how we're to do with less.' A highly comic state

of life for two private gentlemen! but for two nations, it
seems to me, not wholly comic? Bedlam would be comic,
perhaps, if there were only one madman in it; and your
Christmas pantomime is comic, when there is only one clown
in it; but when the whole world turns clown, and paints
itself red with its own heart's blood instead of vermilion, it
is something else than comic, I think.

Mind, I know a great deal of this is play, and willingly
allow for that. You don't know what to do with yourselves
for a sensation: fox-hunting and cricketing will not carry you
through the whole of this unendurably long mortal life: you
liked pop-guns when you were schoolboys, and rifles and
Armstrongs are only the same things better made: but then
the worst of it is, that what was play to you when boys, was
not play to the sparrows; and what is play to you now, is
not play to the small birds of State neither; and for the
black eagles, you are somewhat shy of taking shots at them,
if I mistake not.

I must get back to the matter in hand, however. Believe
me, without farther instance, I could show you, in all time,
that every nation's vice, or virtue, was written in its art : the
soldiership of early Greece ; the sensuality of late Italy ; the
visionary religion of Tuscany; the splendid human energy
and beauty of Venice. I have no time to do this to-night (I
have done it elsewhere before now); but I proceed

to apply the principle to ourselves in a more searching manner.

I notice that among all the new buildings that cover your once wild hills, churches and schools are mixed in due, that is to say, in large proportion, with your mills and mansions and I notice also that the churches and schools are almost always Gothic, and the mansions and mills are never Gothic. Will you allow me to ask precisely the meaning of this? For, remember, it is peculiarly a modern phenomenon. When Gothic was invented, houses were Gothic as well as churches; and when the Italian style superseded the Gothic, churches were Italian as well as houses. If there is a Gothic spire to the cathedral of Antwerp, there is a Gothic belfry to the Hôtel de Ville at Brussels; if Inigo Jones builds an Italian Whitehall, Sir Christopher Wren builds an Italian St. Paul's. But now you live under one school of architecture, and worship under another. What do you mean by doing this? Am I to understand that you are thinking of changing your architecture back to Gothic; and that you treat your churches experimentally, because it does not matter what mistakes you make in a church? Or am I to understand that you consider Gothic a pre-eminently sacred and beautiful mode of building, which you think, like the fine frankincense, should be mixed for the tabernacle only, and reserved for your religious services? For if this be the feeling, though it may seem at first as if it were graceful and reverent, you will find that, at the root of the matter, it signifies neither more nor less than that you have separated your religion from your life.

For consider what a wide significance this fact has; and remember that it is not you only, but all the people of England, who are behaving thus just now.

You have all got into the habit of calling the church 'the house of God.' I have seen, over the doors of many churches, the legend actually carved, ' *This* is the house of God, and this is the gate of heaven.' Now, note where that legend comes from, and of what place it was first spoken. A boy leaves his father's house to go on a long journey on foot, to visit his uncle; he has to cross a wild hill-desert; just as if one of your own boys had to cross the wolds of Westmoreland, to visit an uncle at Carlisle. The second or third day your boy finds himself somewhere between Hawes and Brough, in the midst of the moors, at sunset. It is stony ground, and boggy; he cannot go one foot farther that night. Down he lies, to sleep, on Wharnside, where best he may, gathering a few of the stones together to put under his head;—so wild the place is, he cannot get anything but stones. And there, lying under the broad night, he has a dream; and he sees a ladder set up on the earth, and the top of it reaches to heaven, and the angels of God are ascending

3*

and descending upon it. And when he wakes out of his
sleep, he says, 'How dreadful is this place; surely, this is
none other than the house of God, and this is the gate of
heaven.' This PLACE, observe; not this church; not this
city; not this stone, even, which he puts up for a memorial—
the piece of flint on which his head has lain. But this
place; this windy slope of Wharnside; this moorland hollow, torrent-bitten, snow-blighted; this *any* place where
God lets down the ladder. And how are you to know where
that will be? or how are you to determine where it may be,
but by being ready for it always? Do you know where the
lightning is to fall next? You *do* know that, partly; you
can guide the lightning; but you cannot guide the going
forth of the Spirit, which is that lightning when it shines
from the east to the west.

But the perpetual and insolent warping of that strong
verse to serve a merely ecclesiastical purpose, is only one of
the thousand instances in which we sink back into gross
Judaism. We call our churches 'temples.' Now, you
know, or ought to know, they are *not* temples. They have
never had, never can have, anything whatever to do with
temples. They are 'synagogues'—'gathering places'—
where you gather yourselves together as an assembly; and
by not calling them so, you again miss the force of another
mighty text—'Thou, when thou prayest, shalt not be as the

hypocrites are; for they love to pray standing in the *churches*' [we should translate it], 'that they may be seen of men. But thou, when thou prayest, enter into thy closet, and when thou hast shut thy door, pray to thy Father,'— which is, not in chancel nor in aisle, but ' in secret.'

Now, you feel, as I say this to you—I know you feel—as if I were trying to take away the honour of your churches. Not so; I am trying to prove to you the honour of your houses and your hills; I am trying to show you—not that the Church is not sacred—but that the whole Earth is. I would have you feel, what careless, what constant, what infectious sin there is in all modes of thought, whereby, in calling your churches only ' holy,' you call your hearths and homes profane; and have separated yourselves from the heathen by casting all your household gods to the ground, instead of recognising, in the place of their many and feeble Lares, the presence of your One and Mighty Lord and Lar.

' But what has all this to do with our Exchange ? ' you ask me, impatiently. My dear friends, it has just everything to do with it ; on these inner and great questions depend all the outer and little ones; and if you have asked me down here to speak to you, because you had before been interested in anything I have written, you must know that all I have yet said about architecture was to show this. The book I called ' The Seven Lamps ' was to show that certain right states of temper and moral feeling were the magic powers by which all good architecture, without exception, had been produced. 'The Stones of Venice' had, from beginning to end, no other aim than to show that the Gothic architecture of Venice had arisen out of, and indicated in all its features, a state of pure national faith, and of domestic virtue; and that its Renaissance architecture had arisen out of, and in all its features indicated, a state of concealed national infidelity, and of domestic corruption. And now, you ask me what style is best to build in; and how can I answer, knowing the meaning of the two styles, but by another question—do you mean to build as Christians or as Infidels? And still more—do you mean to build as honest Christians or as honest Infidels? as thoroughly and confessedly either one or the other? You don't like to be asked such rude questions. I cannot help it; they are of much more importance than this Exchange business; and if they can be at once answered, the Exchange business settles itself in a moment. But, before I press them farther, I must ask leave to explain one point clearly. In all my past work, my endeavour has been to show that good architecture is essentially religious—the production of a faithful and virtuous, not of an infidel and corrupted people. But in the course of doing this, I have had also to show that good architecture is not *ecclesiastical*. People are so apt to look upon religion as the business of the clergy, not their own, that the

moment they hear of anything depending on 'religion,' they
think it must also have depended on the priesthood; and I
have had to take what place was to be occupied between
these two errors, and fight both, often with seeming contra-
diction. Good architecture is the work of good and believing men; therefore, you say, at least some people say, 'Good
architecture must essentially have been the work of the clergy, not of the laity.' No—a thousand times no; good architecture has always been the work of the commonalty, *not* of
the clergy. What, you say, those glorious cathedrals—the
pride of Europe—did their builders not form Gothic architecture? No; they corrupted Gothic architecture. Gothic
was formed in the baron's castle, and the burgher's street.
It was formed by the thoughts, and hands, and powers of
free citizens and soldier kings. By the monk it was used as
an instrument for the aid of his superstition; when that superstition became a beautiful madness, and the best hearts of
Europe vainly dreamed and pined in the cloister, and vainly
raged and perished in the crusade—through that fury of per-
verted faith and wasted war, the Gothic rose also to its love-
liest, most fantastic, and, finally, most foolish dreams; and,
in those dreams, was lost.

I hope, now, that there is no risk of your misunderstanding
me when I come to the gist of what I want to say to-night—
when I repeat, that every great national architecture has been

the result and exponent of a great national religion. You can't have bits of it here, bits there—you must have it everywhere, or nowhere. It is not the monopoly of a clerical company—it is not the exponent of a theological dogma—it is not the hieroglyphic writing of an initiated priesthood; it is the manly language of a people inspired by resolute and common purpose, and rendering resolute and common fidelity to the legible laws of an undoubted God.

Now, there have as yet been three distinct schools of European architecture. I say, European, because Asiatic and African architectures belong so entirely to other races and climates, that there is no question of them here; only, in passing, I will simply assure you that whatever is good or great in Egypt, and Syria, and India, is just good or great for the same reasons as the buildings on our side of the Bosphorus. We Europeans, then, have had three great religions: the Greek, which was the worship of the God of Wisdom and Power; the Mediæval, which was the Worship of the God of Judgment and Consolation; the Renaissance, which was the worship of the God of Pride and Beauty; these three we have had—they are past,—and now, at last, we English have got a fourth religion, and a God of our own, about which I want to ask you. But I must explain these three old ones first.

I repeat, first, the Greeks essentially worshipped the God

of Wisdom; so that whatever contended against their religion,—to the Jews a stumbling block,—was, to the Greeks—
Foolishness.

The first Greek idea of Deity was that expressed in the
word, of which we keep the remnant in our words '*Di*-urnal''
and '*Di*-vine'—the god of *Day*, Jupiter the revealer. Athena
is his daughter, but especially daughter of the Intellect,
springing armed from the head. We are only with the help
of recent investigation beginning to penetrate the depth of
meaning couched under the Athenaic symbols: but I may
note rapidly, that her ægis, the mantle with the serpent
fringes, in which she often, in the best statues, is represented
as folding up her left hand for better guard, and the Gorgon
on her shield, are both representative mainly of the chilling
horror and sadness (turning men to stone, as it were,) of the
outmost and superficial spheres of knowledge—that knowledge which separates, in bitterness, hardness, and sorrow,
the heart of the full-grown man from the heart of the child.
For out of imperfect knowledge spring terror, dissension,
danger, and disdain; but from perfect knowledge, given by
the full-revealed Athena, strength and peace, in sign of which
she is crowned with the olive spray, and bears the resistless
spear.

This, then, was the Greek conception of purest Deity,
and every habit of life, and every form of his art developed

themselves from the seeking this bright, serene, resistless wisdom; and setting himself, as a man, to do things evermore rightly and strongly;* not with any ardent affection or ultimate hope; but with a resolute and continent energy of will, as knowing that for failure there was no consolation, and for sin there was no remission. And the Greek architecture rose unerring, bright, clearly defined, and self-contained.

Next followed in Europe the great Christian faith, which was essentially the religion of Comfort. Its great doctrine is the remission of sins; for which cause it happens, too often, in certain phases of Christianity, that sin and sickness themselves are partly glorified, as if, the more you had to be healed of, the more divine was the healing. The practical result of this doctrine, in art, is a continual contemplation of sin and disease, and of imaginary states of purification from them; thus we have an architecture conceived in a

---

* It is an error to suppose that the Greek worship, or seeking, was chiefly of Beauty. It was essentially of Rightness and Strength, founded on Forethought: the principal character of Greek art is not Beauty, but Design: and the Dorian Apollo-worship and Athenian Virgin-worship are both expressions of adoration of divine Wisdom and Purity. Next to these great deities rank, in power over the national mind, Dionysus and Ceres, the givers of human strength and life: then, for heroic example, Hercules. There is no Venus-worship among the Greeks in the great times: and the Muses are essentially teachers of Truth, and of its harmonies.

mingled sentiment of melancholy and aspiration, partly severe, partly luxuriant, which will bend itself to every one of our needs, and every one of our fancies, and be strong or weak with us, as we are strong or weak ourselves. It is, of all architecture, the basest, when base people build it—of all, the noblest, when built by the noble.

And now note that both these religions—Greek and Mediæval—perished by falsehood in their own main purpose. The Greek religion of Wisdom perished in a false philosophy —'Oppositions of science, falsely so called.' The Mediæval religion of Consolation perished in false comfort; in remission of sins given lyingly. It was the selling of absolution that ended the Mediæval faith; and I can tell you more, it is the selling of absolution which, to the end of time, will mark false Christianity. Pure Christianity gives her remission of sins only by *ending* them; but false Christianity gets her remission of sins by *compounding for* them. And there are many ways of compounding for them. We English have beautiful little quiet ways of buying absolution, whether in low Church or high, far more cunning than any of Tetzel's trading.

Then, thirdly, there followed the religion of Pleasure, in which all Europe gave itself to luxury, ending in death. First, *bals masqués* in every saloon, and then guillotines in every square. And all these three worships issue in vast temple building. Your Greek worshipped Wisdom, and

built you the Parthenon—the Virgin's temple. The Mediæval worshipped Consolation, and built you Virgin temples
also—but to our Lady of Salvation. Then the Revivalist
worshipped beauty, of a sort, and built you Versailles, and
the Vatican. Now, lastly, will you tell me what *we* worship,
and what *we* build?

You know we are speaking always of the real, active, continual, national worship; that by which men act while they
live; not that which they talk of when they die. Now, we
have, indeed, a nominal religion, to which we pay tithes of
property and sevenths of time; but we have also a practical
and earnest religion, to which we devote nine-tenths of our
property and sixth-sevenths of our time. And we dispute a
great deal about the nominal religion; but we are all unanimous about this practical one, of which I think you will admit
that the ruling goddess may be best generally described as
the 'Goddess of Getting-on,' or 'Britannia of the Market.'
The Athenians had an 'Athena Agoraia,' or Minerva of the
Market; but she was a subordinate type of their goddess,
while our Britannia Agoraia is the principal type of ours.
And all your great architectural works, are, of course, built
to her. It is long since you built a great cathedral; and how
you would laugh at me, if I proposed building a cathedral on
the top of one of these hills of yours, taking it for an Acro-
polis! But your railroad mounds, prolonged masses of Acro-

polis; your railroad stations, vaster than the Parthenon, and innumerable; your chimneys, how much more mighty and costly than cathedral spires! your harbour-piers; your warehouses; your exchanges!—all these are built to your great Goddess of 'Getting-on;' and she has formed, and will continue to form, your architecture, as long as you worship her; and it is quite vain to ask me to tell you how to build to *her;* you know far better than I.

There might indeed, on some theories, be a conceivably good architecture for Exchanges—that is to say if there were any heroism in the fact or deed of exchange, which might be typically carved on the outside of your building. For, you know, all beautiful architecture must be adorned with sculpture or painting; and for sculpture or painting, you must have a subject. And hitherto it has been a received opinion among the nations of the world that the only right subjects for either, were *heroisms* of some sort. Even on his pots and his flagons, the Greek put a Hercules slaying lions, or an Apollo slaying serpents, or Bacchus slaying melancholy giants, and earth-born despondencies. On his temples, the Greek put contests of great warriors in founding states, or of gods with evil spirits. On his houses and temples alike, the Christian put carvings of angels conquering devils; or of hero-martyrs exchanging this world for another; subject inappropriate, I think, to our manner of exchange here. And

the Master of Christians not only left his followers without
any orders as to the sculpture of affairs of exchange on the
outside of buildings, but gave some strong evidence of his
dislike of affairs of exchange within them. And yet there
might surely be a heroism in such affairs; and all commerce
become a kind of selling of doves, not impious. The wonder
has always been great to me, that heroism has never been
supposed to be in anywise consistent with the practice of
supplying people with food, or clothes; but rather with that
of quartering oneself upon them for food, and stripping them
of their clothes. Spoiling of armour is an heroic deed in all
ages; but the selling of clothes, old, or new, has never taken
any colour of magnanimity. Yet one does not see why feeding the hungry and clothing the naked should ever become
base businesses, even when engaged in on a large scale. If
one could contrive to attach the notion of conquest to them
anyhow? so that, supposing there were anywhere an obsti-
nate race, who refused to be comforted, one might take some
pride in giving them compulsory comfort; and as it were,
'occupying a country' with one's gifts, instead of one's
armies? If one could only consider it as much a victory to
get a barren field sown, as to get an eared field stripped; and
contend who should build villages, instead of who should
'carry' them. Are not all forms of heroism, conceivable in
doing these serviceable deeds? You doubt who is strongest?

It might be ascertained by push of spade, as well as push of
sword. Who is wisest? There are witty things to be
thought of in planning other business than campaigns. Who
is bravest? There are always the elements to fight with,
stronger than men; and nearly as merciless. The only
absolutely and unapproachably heroic element in the soldier's
work seems to be—that he is paid little for it—and regularly:
while you traffickers, and exchangers, and others occupied in
presumably benevolent business, like to be paid much for it—
and by chance. I never can make out how it is that a
knight-errant does not expect to be paid for his trouble, but
a pedlar-errant always does;—that people are willing to take
hard knocks for nothing, but never to sell ribands cheap;—
that they are ready to go on fervent crusades to recover the
tomb of a buried God, never on any travels to fulfil the
orders of a living God;—that they will go anywhere barefoot
to preach their faith, but must be well bribed to practise it,
and are perfectly ready to give the Gospel gratis, but never
the loaves and fishes. If you chose to take the matter up on
any such soldierly principle, to do your commerce, and your
feeding of nations, for fixed salaries; and to be as particular
about giving people the best food, and the best cloth, as
soldiers are about giving them the best gunpowder, I could
carve something for you on your exchange worth looking at.
But I can only at present suggest decorating its frieze with

pendant purses; and making its pillars broad at the base, for the sticking of bills. And in the innermost chambers of it there might be a statue of Britannia of the Market, who may have, perhaps advisably, a partridge for her crest, typical at once of her courage in fighting for noble ideas; and of her interest in game; and round its neck the inscription in golden letters, 'Perdix fovit quæ non peperit.' * Then, for her spear, she might have a weaver's beam; and on her shield, instead of her Cross, the Milanese boar, semi-fleeced, with the town of Gennesaret proper, in the field and the legend ' In the best market,' and her corslet, of leather, folded over her heart in the shape of a purse, with thirty slits in it for a piece of money to go in at, on each day of the month. And I doubt not but that people would come to see your exchange, and its goddess, with applause.

Nevertheless, I want to point out to you certain strange characters in this goddess of yours. She differs from the great Greek and Mediæval deities essentially in two things— first, as to the continuance of her presumed power; secondly, as to the extent of it.

1st, as to the Continuance.

* Jerem. xvii. 11 (best in Septuagint and Vulgate). ' As the partridge, fostering what she brought not forth, so he that getteth riches, not by right, shall leave them in the midst of his days, and at his end shall be a fool.'

The Greek Goddess of Wisdom gave continual increase of wisdom, as the Christian Spirit of Comfort (or Comforter) continual increase of comfort. There was no question, with these, of any limit or cessation of function. But with your Agora Goddess, that is just the most important question. Getting on—but where to? Gathering together—but how much? Do you mean to gather always—never to spend? If so, I wish you joy of your goddess, for I am just as well off as you, without the trouble of worshipping her at all. But if you do not spend, somebody else will—somebody else must. And it is because of this (among many other such errors) that I have fearlessly declared your so-called science of Political Economy to be no science; because, namely, it has omitted the study of exactly the most important branch of the business—the study of *spending*. For spend you must, and as much as you make, ultimately. You gather corn:—will you bury England under a heap of grain; or will you, when you have gathered, finally eat? You gather gold:—will you make your house-roofs of it, or pave your streets with it? That is still one way of spending it. But if you keep it, that you may get more, I'll give you more; I'll give you all the gold you want—all you can imagine— if you can tell me what you'll do with it. You shall have thousands of gold pieces;—thousands of thousands—millions —mountains, of gold: where will you keep them? Will you put an Olympus of silver upon a golden Pelion—make Ossa like a wart? Do you think the rain and dew would then come down to you, in the streams from such mountains, more blessedly than they will down the mountains which God has made for you, of moss and whinstone? But it is not gold that you want to gather! What is it? green-backs? No; not those neither. What is it then—is it ciphers after a capital I? Cannot you practise writing ciphers, and write as many as you want? Write ciphers for an hour every morning, in a big book, and say every even-ing, I am worth all those noughts more than I was yester-day. Won't that do? Well, what in the name of Plutus is it you want? Not gold, not greenbacks, not ciphers after a capital I? You will have to answer, after all, 'No; we want, somehow or other, money's *worth.*' Well, what is that? Let your Goddess of Getting-on discover it, and let her learn to stay therein.

II. But there is yet another question to be asked respect-ing this Goddess of Getting-on. The first was of the con-tinuance of her power; the second is of its extent.

Pallas and the Madonna were supposed to be all the world's Pallas, and all the world's Madonna. They could teach all men, and they could comfort all men. But, look strictly into the nature of the power of your Goddess of Getting-on; and you will find she is the Goddess—not of everybody's getting on—but only of somebody's getting on. This is a vital, or rather deathful, distinction. Examine it in your own ideal of the state of national life which this Goddess is to evoke and maintain. I asked you what it was, when I was last here;*—you have never told me. Now, shall I try to tell you?

Your ideal of human life then is, I think, that it should be passed in a pleasant undulating world, with iron and coal everywhere underneath it. On each pleasant bank of this world is to be a beautiful mansion, with two wings; and stables, and coach-houses; a moderately sized park; a large garden and hot-houses; and pleasant carriage drives through the shrubberies. In this mansion are to live the favoured votaries of the Goddess; the English gentleman, with his gracious wife, and his beautiful family; always able to have the boudoir and the jewels for the wife, and the beautiful ball dresses for the daughters, and hunters for the sons, and a shooting in the Highlands for himself. At the bottom of the bank, is to be the mill; not less than a quarter of a mile long, with a steam engine at each end, and two in the middle, and a chimney three hundred feet high. In this mill are to be in constant employment from eight hundred to a thousand workers, who never drink, never strike, always go to

* Two Paths, p. 98.
4

church on Sunday, and always express themselves in respect
ful language.

Is not that, broadly, and in the main features, the kind of
thing you propose to yourselves? It is very pretty indeed
seen from above; not at all so pretty, seen from below.
For, observe, while to one family this deity is indeed the
Goddess of Getting on, to a thousand families she is the
Goddess of *not* Getting on. 'Nay,' you say, 'they have all
their chance.' Yes, so has every one in a lottery, but there
must always be the same number of blanks. 'Ah! but in
a lottery it is not skill and intelligence which take the lead,
but blind chance.' What then! do you think the old
practice, that 'they should take who have the power, and
they should keep who can,' is less iniquitous, when the
power has become power of brains instead of fist? and
that, though we may not take advantage of a child's or a
woman's weakness, we may of a man's foolishness? 'Nay,
but finally, work must be done, and some one must be at the
top, some one at the bottom.' Granted, my friends. Work
must always be, and captains of work must always be; and
if you in the least remember the tone of any of my writings,
you must know that they are thought unfit for this age,
because they are always insisting on need of government,
and speaking with scorn of liberty. But I beg you to
observe that there is a wide difference between being

captains or governors of work, and taking the profits of it. It does not follow, because you are general of an army, that you are to take all the treasure, or land, it wins (if it fight for treasure or land); neither, because you are king of a nation, that you are to consume all the profits of the nation's work. Real kings, on the contrary, are known invariably by their doing quite the reverse of this,—by their taking the least possible quantity of the nation's work for themselves. There is no test of real kinghood so infallible as that. Does the crowned creature live simply, bravely, unostentatiously? probably he *is* a King. Does he cover his body with jewels, and his table with delicates? in all probability he is *not* a King. It is possible he may be, as Solomon was; but that is when the nation shares his splendour with him. Solomon made gold, not only to be in his own palace as stones, but to be in Jerusalem as stones. But even so, for the most part, these splendid kinghoods expire in ruin, and only the true kinghoods live, which are of royal labourers governing loyal labourers; who, both leading rough lives, establish the true dynasties. Conclusively you will find that because you are king of a nation, it does not follow that you are to gather for yourself all the wealth of that nation; neither, because you are king of a small part of the nation, and lord over the means of its maintenance—over field, or mill, or mine, are you to take all the produce of

that piece of the foundation of national existence for
yourself.

You will tell me I need not preach against these things,
for I cannot mend them. No, good friends, I cannot; but
you can, and you will; or something else can and will. Do
you think these phenomena are to stay always in their pre
sent power or aspect? All history shows, on the contrary,
that to be the exact thing they never can do. Change
must come; but it is ours to determine whether change of
growth, or change of death. Shall the Parthenon be in ruins
on its rock, and Bolton priory in its meadow, but these mills
of yours be the consummation of the buildings of the earth,
and their wheels be as the wheels of eternity? Think you
that 'men may come, and men may go,' but—mills—go on
for ever? Not so; out of these, better or worse shall come;
and it is for you to choose which.

I know that none of this wrong is done with deliberate
purpose. I know, on the contrary, that you wish your workmen well; that you do much for them, and that you desire to
do more for them, if you saw your way to it safely. I know
that many of you have done, and are every day doing, whatever you feel to be in your power; and that even all this
wrong and misery are brought about by a warped sense of
duty, each of you striving to do his best, without noticing
that this best is essentially and centrally the best for himself,

not for others. And all this has come of the spreading of that thrice accursed, thrice impious doctrine of the modern economist, that 'To do the best for yourself, is finally to do the best for others.' Friends, our great Master said not so; and most absolutely we shall find this world is not made so. Indeed, to do the best for others, is finally to do the best for ourselves; but it will not do to have our eyes fixed on that issue. The Pagans had got beyond that. Hear what a Pagan says of this matter; hear what were, perhaps, the last written words of Plato,—if not the last actually written (for this we cannot know), yet assuredly in fact and power his parting words—in which, endeavouring to give full crowning and harmonious close to all his thoughts, and to speak the sum of them by the imagined sentence of the Great Spirit, his strength and his heart fail him, and the words cease, broken off for ever. It is the close of the dialogue called 'Critias,' in which he describes, partly from real tradition, partly in ideal dream, the early state of Athens; and the genesis, and order, and religion, of the fabled isle of Atlantis; in which genesis he conceives the same first perfection and final degeneracy of man, which in our own Scriptural tradition is expressed by saying that the Sons of God intermarried with the daughters of men, for he supposes the earliest race to have been indeed the children of God; and to have corrupted themselves, until 'their spot was not the spot of his children.'

And this, he says, was the end; that indeed 'through many
generations, so long as the God's nature in them yet was full,
they were submissive to the sacred laws, and carried themselves lovingly to all that had kindred with them in divine-
ness; for their uttermost spirit was faithful and true, and in
every wise great; so that, in all meekness of wisdom, they
dealt with each other, and took all the chances of life; and despising all things except virtue, they cared little what hap-
pened day by day, and *bore lightly the burden* of gold and of
possessions; for they saw that, if only their common love
and virtue increased, all these things would be increased together with them; but to set their esteem and ardent pursuit upon material possession would be to lose that first, and
their virtue and affection together with it.   And by such
reasoning, and what of the divine nature remained in them,
they gained all this greatness of which we have already told;
but when the God's part of them faded and became extinct,
being mixed again and again, and effaced by the prevalent
mortality; and the human nature at last exceeded, they then
became unable to endure the courses of fortune; and fell into
shapelessness of life, and baseness in the sight of him who
could see, having lost everything that was fairest of their honour; while to the blind hearts which could not discern the
true life, tending to happiness, it seemed that they were then
chiefly noble and happy, being filled with all iniquity of inor-

dinate possession and power. Whereupon, the God of Gods, whose Kinghood is in laws, beholding a once just nation thus cast into misery, and desiring to lay such punishment upon them as might make them repent into restraining, gathered together all the gods into his dwelling-place, which from heaven's centre overlooks whatever has part in creation; and having assembled them, he said'——

The rest is silence. So ended are the last words of the chief wisdom of the heathen, spoken of this idol of riches; this idol of yours; this golden image high by measureless cubits, set up where your green fields of England are furnace-burnt into the likeness of the plain of Dura : this idol, forbidden to us, first of all idols, by our own Master and faith; forbidden to us also by every human lip that has ever, in any age or people, been accounted of as able to speak according to the purposes of God. Continue to make that forbidden deity your principal one, and soon no more art, no more science, no more pleasure will be possible. Catastrophe will come; or worse than catastrophe, slow mouldering and withering into Hades. But if you can fix some conception of a true human state of life to be.striven for—life for all men as for yourselves—if you can determine some honest and simple order of existence; following those trodden ways of wisdom, which are pleasantness, and seeking her quiet and withdrawn paths, which are peace ;—then, and so sanctifying wealth into 'commonwealth,' all your art, your literature, your daily labours, your domestic affection, and citizen's duty, will join and increase into one magnificent harmony. You will know then how to build, well enough; you will build with stone well, but with flesh better; temples not made with hands, but riveted of hearts; and that kind of marble, crimson-veined, is indeed eternal.

WAR.

LECTURE III.

(*Delivered at the Royal Military Academy, Woolwich.*)

WAR.

YOUNG SOLDIERS, I do not doubt but that many of you came
unwillingly to-night, and many in merely contemptuous
curiosity, to hear what a writer on painting could possibly
say, or would venture to say, respecting your great art of
war. You may well think within yourselves, that a painter
might, perhaps without immodesty, lecture younger painters
upon painting, but not young lawyers upon law, nor young
physicians upon medicine — least of all, it may seem to you,
young warriors upon war. And, indeed, when I was asked
to address you, I declined at first, and declined long; for I
felt that you would not be interested in my special business,
and would certainly think there was small need for me to
come to teach you yours. Nay, I knew that there ought
to be *no* such need, for the great veteran soldiers of England are now men every way so thoughtful, so noble, and so
good, that no other teaching than their knightly example, and
their few words of grave and tried counsel should be either

necessary for you, or even, without assurance of due modesty in the offerer, endured by you.

But being asked, not once nor twice, I have not ventured persistently to refuse; and I will try, in very few words, to lay before you some reason why you should accept my xcuse, and hear me patiently. You may imagine that your work is wholly foreign to, and separate from mine. So far from that, all the pure and noble arts of peace are founded on war; no great art ever yet rose on earth, but among a nation of soldiers. There is no art among a shepherd people, if it remains at peace. There is no art among an agricultural people, if it remains at peace. Commerce is barely consistent with fine art; but cannot produce it. Manufacture not only is unable to produce it, but invariably destroys whatever seeds of it exist. There is no great art possible to a nation but that which is based on battle.

Now, though I hope you love fighting for its own sake, you must, I imagine, be surprised at my assertion that there is any such good fruit of fighting. You supposed, probably, that your office was to defend the works of peace, but certainly not to found them: nay, the common course of war, you may have thought, was only to destroy them. And truly, I who tell you this of the use of war, should have been the last of men to tell you so, had I trusted my own experience only. Hear why: I have given a considerable part of my life to the investigation of Venetian painting; and the result of that enquiry was my fixing upon one man as the greatest of all Venetians, and therefore, as I believed, of all painters whatsoever. I formed this faith, (whether right or wrong matters at present nothing,) in the supremacy of the painter Tintoret, under a roof covered with his pictures; and of those pictures, three of the noblest were then in the form of shreds of ragged canvas, mixed up with the laths of the roof, rent through by three Austrian shells. Now it is not every lecturer who *could* tell you that he had seen three of his favourite pictures torn to rags by bomb-shells. And after such a sight, it is not every lecturer who *would* tell you that, nevertheless, war was the foundation of all great art.

Yet the conclusion is inevitable, from any careful comparison of the states of great historic races at different periods. Merely to show you what I mean, I will sketch for you, very briefly, the broad steps of the advance of the best art of the world. The first dawn of it is in Egypt; and the power of it is founded on the perpetual contemplation of death, and of future judgment, by the mind of a nation of which the ruling caste were priests, and the second, soldiers The greatest works produced by them are sculptures of their kings going out to battle, or receiving the homage of conquered armies. And you must remember also, as one of the great keys to the splendour of the Egyptian nation, that the priests were not occupied in theology only. Their theology was the basis of practical government and law; so that they were not so much priests as religious judges: the office of Samuel, among the Jews, being as nearly as possible correspondent to theirs.

All the rudiments of art then, and much more than the rudiments of all science, are laid first by this great warrior-nation, which held in contempt all mechanical trades, and in absolute hatred the peaceful life of shepherds. From Egypt art passes directly into Greece, where all poetry, and all painting, are nothing else than the description, praise, or dramatic representation of war, or of the exercises which prepare for it, in their connection with offices of religion. All Greek institutions had first respect to war; and their conception of it, as one necessary office of all human and divine life, is expressed simply by the images of their guiding gods. Apollo is the god of all wisdom of the intellect; he bears the arrow and the bow, before he bears the lyre. Again, Athena is the goddess of all wisdom in conduct. It is by the helmet and the shield, oftener than by the shuttle, that she is distinguished from other deities.

There were, however, two great differences in principle between the Greek and the Egyptian theories of policy. In Greece there was no soldier caste; every citizen was necessarily a soldier. And, again, while the Greeks rightly despised mechanical arts as much as the Egyptians, they did not make the fatal mistake of despising agricultural and pastoral life; but perfectly honoured both. These two conditions of truer thought raise them quite into the highest rank of wise manhood that has yet been reached; for all our great arts, and nearly all our great thoughts, have been borrowed or derived from them. Take away from us what they have given; and I hardly can imagine how low the modern European would stand.

Now, you are to remember, in passing to the next phase of history, that though you *must* have war to produce art— you must also have much more than war; namely, an art-instinct or genius in the people; and that, though all the talent for painting in the world won't make painters of you, unless you have a gift for fighting as well, you may have the gift for fighting, and none for painting. Now, in the next great dynasty of soldiers, the art-instinct is wholly wanting. I have not yet investigated the Roman character enough to tell you the causes of this; but I believe, paradoxical as it may seem to you, that, however truly the Roman might say of himself that he was born of Mars, and suckled by the wolf, he was nevertheless, at heart, more of a farmer than a soldier. The exercises of war were with him practical, not poetical; his poetry was in domestic life only, and the object

of battle, 'pacis imponere morem.' And the arts are extin
guished in his hands, and do not rise again, until, with
Gothic chivalry, there comes back into the mind of Europe a
passionate delight in war itself, for the sake of war. And
then, with the romantic knighthood which can imagine no
other noble employment,—under the fighting kings of
France, England, and Spain ; and under the fighting dukeships
and citizenships of Italy, art is born again, and rises to her
height in the great valleys of Lombardy and Tuscany, through
which there flows not a single stream, from all their Alps or
Apennines, that did not once run dark red from battle : and it
reaches its culminating glory in the city which gave to history
the most intense type of soldiership yet seen among men ;—the
city whose armies were led in their assault by their king, led
through it to victory by their king, and so led, though that
king of theirs was blind, and in the extremity of his age.

And from this time forward, as peace is established or
extended in Europe, the arts decline. They reach an
unparalleled pitch of costliness, but lose their life, enlist
themselves at last on the side of luxury and various corruption, and, among wholly tranquil nations, wither utterly
away ; remaining only in partial practice among races who,
like the French and us, have still the minds, though we cannot all live the lives, of soldiers.

'It may be so,' I can suppose that a philanthropist might

exclaim. 'Perish then the arts, if they can flourish only at such a cost. What worth is there in toys of canvas and stone, if compared to the joy and peace of artless domestic life?' And the answer is—truly, in themselves, none. But as expressions of the highest state of the human spirit, their worth is infinite. As results they may be worthless, but, as signs, they are above price. For it is an assured truth that, whenever the faculties of men are at their fulness, they *must* express themselves by art; and to say that a state is without such expression, is to say that it is sunk from its proper level of manly nature. So that, when I tell you that war is the foundation of all the arts, I mean also that it is the foundation of all the high virtues and faculties of men. ·

It was very strange to me to discover this; and very dreadful—but I saw it to be quite an undeniable fact. The common notion that peace and the virtues of civil life flourished together, I found, to be wholly untenable. Peace and the *vices* of civil life only flourish together. We talk of peace and learning, and of peace and plenty, and of peace and civilisation; but I found that those were not the words which the Muse of History coupled together: that on her lips, the words were—peace and sensuality, peace and selfishness, peace and corruption, peace and death. I found, in brief, that all great nations learned their truth of word, and strength of thought, in war; that they were nourished in war, and wasted by peace;

taught by war, and deceived by peace; trained by war, and betrayed by peace;—in a word, that they were born in war, and expired in peace.

Yet now note carefully, in the second place, it is not *all* war of which this can be said—nor all dragon's teeth, which, sown, will start up into men. It is not the ravage of a barbarian wolf-flock, as under Genseric or Suwarrow; nor the habitual restlessness and rapine of mountaineers, as on the old borders of Scotland; nor the occasional struggle of a strong peaceful nation for its life, as in the wars of the Swiss with Austria; nor the contest of merely ambitious nations for extent of power, as in the wars of France under Napoleon, or the just terminated war in America. None of these forms of war build anything but tombs. But the creative or foundational war is that in which the natural restlessness and love of contest among men are disciplined, by consent, into modes of beautiful—though it may be fatal—play: in which the natural ambition and love of power of men are disciplined into the aggressive conquest of surrounding evil: and in which the natural instincts of self-defence are sanctified by the nobleness of the institutions, and purity of the households, which they are appointed to defend. To such war as this all men are born; in such war as this any man may happily die; and forth from such war as this have arisen throughout the extent of past ages, all the highest sanctities and virtues of humanity.

1 shall therefore divide the war of which I would speak to you into three heads. War for exercise or play; war for dominion ; and, war for defence.

I. And first, of war for exercise or play. I speak of it primarily in this light, because, through all past history, manly war has been more an exercise than anything else, among the classes who cause, and proclaim it. It is not a game to the conscript, or the pressed sailor; but neither of these are the causers of it. To the governor who determines that war shall be, and to the youths who voluntarily adopt it as their profession, it has always been a grand pastime ; and chiefly pursued because they had nothing else to do. And this is true without any exception. No king whose mind was fully occupied with the development of the inner resources of his kingdom, or with any other sufficing subject of thought, ever entered into war but on compulsion. No youth who was earnestly busy with any peaceful subject of study, or set on any serviceable course of action, ever voluntarily became a soldier. Occupy him early, and wisely, in agriculture or business, in science or in literature, and he will never think of war otherwise than as a calamity. But leave him idle; and, the more brave and active and capable he is by nature, the more he will thirst for some appointed field for action ; and find, in the passion and peril of battle, the only satisfying fulfilment of his unoccupied being. And from the earliest incipient civil-

isation until now, the population of the earth divides itself,
when you look at it widely, into two races; one of workers,
and the other of players—one tilling the ground, manufacturing, building, and otherwise providing for the necessities of
life;—the other part proudly idle, and continually therefore
needing recreation, in which they use the productive and
laborious orders partly as their cattle, and partly as their
puppets or pieces in the game of death.

Now, remember, whatever virtue or goodliness there may
be in this game of war, rightly played, there is none when
you thus play it with a multitude of small human pawns.

If you, the gentlemen of this or any other kingdom,
choose to make your pastime of contest, do so, and welcome;
but set not up these unhappy peasant-pieces upon the green
fielded board. If the wager is to be of death, lay it on your
own heads, not theirs. A goodly struggle in the Olympic
dust, though it be the dust of the grave, the gods will look
upon, and be with you in; but they will not be with you, if
you sit on the sides of the amphitheatre, whose steps are
the mountains of earth, whose arena its valleys, to urge your
peasant millions into gladiatorial war. You also, you tender
and delicate women, for whom, and by whose command, all
true battle has been, and must ever be; you would perhaps
shrink now, though you need not, from the thought of
sitting as queens above set lists where the jousting game

might be mortal. How much more, then, ought you to shrink from the thought of sitting above a theatre pit in which even a few condemned slaves were slaying each other only for your delight! And do you *not* shrink from the *fact* of sitting above a theatre pit, where,—not condemned slaves, —but the best and bravest of the poor sons of your people, slay each other,—not man to man,—as the coupled gladiators; but race to race, in duel of generations? You would tell me, perhaps, that you do not sit to see this; and it is indeed true, that the women of Europe—those who have no heart-interest of their own at peril in the contest—draw the curtains of their boxes, and muffle the openings; so that from the pit of the circus of slaughter there may reach them only at intervals a half-heard cry and a murmur as of the wind's sighing, when myriads of souls expire. They shut out the death-cries; and are happy, and talk wittily among themselves. That is the utter literal fact of what our ladies do in their pleasant lives.

Nay, you might answer, speaking for them—'We do not let these wars come to pass for our play, nor by our carelessness; we cannot help them. How can any final quarrel of nations be settled otherwise than by war?' I cannot now delay, to tell you how political quarrels might be otherwise settled.. But grant that they cannot. Grant that no law of reason can be understood by nations; no law of justice submitted to by them: and that, while questions of a few acres, and of petty cash, can be determined by truth and equity, the questions which are to issue in the perishing or saving of kingdoms can be determined only by the truth of the sword, and the equity of the rifle. Grant this, and even then, judge if it will always be necessary for you to put your quarrel into the hearts of your poor, and sign your treaties with peasants' blood. You would be ashamed to do this in your own private position and power. Why should you not be ashamed also to do it in public place and power? If you quarrel with your neighbour, and the quarrel be indeterminable by law, and mortal, you and he do not send your footmen to Battersea fields to fight it out; nor do you set fire to his tenants' cottages, nor spoil their goods. You fight out your quarrel yourselves, and at your own danger, if at all. And you do not think it materially affects the arbitrement that one of you has a larger household than the other; so that, if the servants or tenants were brought into the field with their masters, the issue of the contest could not be doubtful? You either refuse the private duel, or you practise it under laws of honour, not of physical force; that so it may be, in a manner, justly concluded. Now the just or unjust conclusion of the private feud is of little moment, while the just or unjust conclusion of the public feud is of eternal moment: and yet, in this public quarrel, you take your servants' sons from their arms

to fight for it, and your servants' food from their lips to support it; and the black seals on the parchment of your treaties
of peace are the deserted hearth and the fruitless field.
There is a ghastly ludicrousness in this, as there is mostly in
these wide and universal crimes. Hear the statement of the
very fact of it in the most literal words of the greatest of our
English thinkers:—

'What, speaking in quite unofficial language, is the net-purport and
upshot of war? To my own knowledge, for example, there dwell
and toil, in the British village of Dumdrudge, usually some five hundred souls. From these, by certain "natural enemies" of the French,
there are successively selected, during the French war, say thirty able-
bodied men. Dumdrudge, at her own expense, has suckled and
nursed them; she has, not without difficulty and sorrow, fed them up
to manhood, and even trained them to crafts, so that one can weave,
another build, another hammer, and the weakest can stand under
thirty stone avoirdupois. Nevertheless, amid much weeping and
swearing, they are selected; all dressed in red; and shipped away, at
the public charges, some two thousand miles, or say only to the south
of Spain; and fed there till wanted.

'And now to that same spot in the south of Spain are thirty similar
French artisans, from a French Dumdrudge, in like manner wending;
till at length, after infinite effort, the two parties come into actual
juxtaposition; and Thirty stands fronting Thirty, each with a gun in
his hand.

'Straightway the word "Fire!" is given, and they blow the souls out of one another, and in place of sixty brisk useful craftsmen, the world has sixty dead carcas s, which it must bury, and anon shed tears for. Had these men any quarrel? Busy as the devil is, not the smallest! They lived far enough apart; were the entirest strangers; nay, in so wide a universe, there was even, unconsciously, by commerce, some mutual helpfulness between them. How then? Simpleton! their governors had fallen out; and instead of shooting one another, had the cunning to make these poor blockheads shoot.' (Sartor Resartus.)

Positively, then, gentlemen, the game of battle must not, and shall not, ultimately be played this way. But should it be played any way? Should it, if not by your servants, be practised by yourselves? I think, yes. Both history and human instinct seem alike to say, yes. All healthy men like fighting, and like the sense of danger; all brave women like to hear of their fighting, and of their facing danger. This is a fixed instinct in the fine race of them; and I cannot help fancying that fair fight is the best play for them; and that a tournament was a better game than a steeple-chase. The time may perhaps come in France as well as here, for universal hurdle-races and cricketing: but I do not think universal 'crickets' will bring out the best qualities of the nobles of either country. I use, in such question, the test which I have adopted, of the connection of war with other arts; and I reflect how, as a sculptor, I should feel, if I were asked to

design a monument for a dead knight, in Westminster abbey,
with a carving of a bat at one end, and a ball at the other.
It may be the remains in me only of savage Gothic prejudice;
but I had rather carve it with a shield at one end, and a
sword at the other. And this, observe, with no reference
whatever to any story of duty done, or cause defended.
Assume the knight merely to have ridden out occasionally to
fight his neighbour for exercise; assume him even a soldier
of fortune, and to have gained his bread, and filled his purse,
at the sword's point. Still, I feel as if it were, somehow,
grander and worthier in him to have made his bread by
sword play than any other play; I had rather he had made it
by thrusting than by batting;—much more, than by betting.
Much rather that he should ride war horses, than back race
horses; and—I say it sternly and deliberately—much
rather would I have him slay his neighbour, than cheat
him.

But remember, so far as this may be true, the game
of war is only that in which the *full personal power of
the human creature* is brought out in management of its
weapons. And this for three reasons :—

First, the great justification of this game is that it truly
when well played, determines *who is the best man ;—*
who is the highest bred, the most self-denying, the most
fearless, the coolest of nerve, the swiftest of eye and hand.

5

You cannot test these qualities wholly, unless there is a clear possibility of the struggle's ending in death. It is only in the fronting of that condition that the full trial of the man, soul and body, comes out. You may go to your game of wickets, or of hurdles, or of cards, and any knavery that is in you may stay unchallenged all the while. But if the play may be ended at any moment by a lance-thrust, a man will probably make up his accounts a little before he enters it. Whatever is rotten and evil in him will weaken his hand more in holding a sword hilt, than in balancing a billiard cue; and on the whole, the habit of living lightly hearted, in daily presence of death, always has had, and must have, a tendency both to the making and testing of honest men. But for the final testing, observe, you must make the issue of battle strictly dependent on fineness of frame, and firmness of hand. You must not make it the question, which of the combatants has the longest gun, or which has got behind the biggest tree, or which has the wind in his face, or which has gunpowder made by the best chemists, or iron smelted with the best coal, or the angriest mob at his back. Decide your battle, whether of nations, or individuals, on *those* terms;—and you have only multiplied confusion, and added slaughter to iniquity. But decide your battle by pure trial which has the strongest arm, and steadiest heart,—and you have gone far to decide a great many matters besides, and to decide them rightly.

And the other reasons for this mode of decision of cause, are the diminution both of the material destructiveness, or cost, and of the physical distress of war. For you must not think that in speaking to you in this (as you may imagine), fantastic praise of battle, I have overlooked the conditions weighing against me. I pray all of you, who have not read, to read with the most earnest attention, Mr. Helps's two essays on War and Government, in the first volume of the last series of 'Friends in Council.' Everything that can be urged against war is there simply, exhaustively, and most graphically stated. And all, there urged, is true. But the two great counts of evil alleged against war by that most thoughtful writer, hold only against modern war. If you have to take away masses of men from all industrial employment,—to feed them by the labour of others,—to move them and provide them with destructive machines, varied daily in national rivalship of inventive cost; if you have to ravage the country which you attack,—to destroy for a score of future years, its roads, its woods, its cities, and its harbours;—and if, finally, having brought masses of men, counted by hundreds of thousands, face to face, you tear those masses to pieces with jagged shot, and leave the fragments of living creatures, countlessly beyond all help of

surgery, to starve and parch, through days of torture, down
into clots of clay—what book of accounts shall record the
cost of your work;—What book of judgment sentence the
guilt of it?

That, I say, is *modern* war,—scientific war,—chemical and
mechanic war, worse even than the savage's poisoned arrow.
And yet you will tell me, perhaps, that any other war than this
is impossible now. It may be so ; the progress of science cannot, perhaps, be otherwise registered than by new facilities
of destruction ; and the brotherly love of our enlarging
Christianity be only proved by multiplication of murder.
Yet hear, for a moment, what war was, in Pagan and igno-
rant days ;—what war might yet be, if we could extinguish
our science in darkness, and join the heathen's practice to the
Christian's theory. I read you this from a book which probably most of you know well, and all ought to know—Muller's
' Dorians ; '—but I have put the points I wish you to remember in closer connection than in his text.

'The chief characteristic of the warriors of Sparta was
great composure and subdued strength ; the violence (λύσσα)
of Aristodemus and Isadas being considered as deserving
rather of blame than praise ; and these qualities in general
distinguished the Greeks from the northern Barbarians, whose
boldness always consisted in noise and tumult. For the same
reason the Spartans *sacrificed to the Muses* before an action ;

these goddesses being expected to produce regularity and order in battle; as they *sacrificed on the same occasion in Crete to the god of love,* as the confirmer of mutual esteem and shame. Every man put on a crown, when the band of flute-players gave the signal for attack; all the shields of the line glittered with their high polish, and mingled their splendour with the dark red of the purple mantles, which were meant both to adorn the combatant, and to conceal the blood of the wounded; to fall well and decorously being an incentive the more to the most heroic valour. The conduct of the Spartans in battle denotes a high and noble disposition, which rejected all the extremes of brutal rage. The pursuit of the enemy ceased when the victory was completed; and after the signal for retreat had been given, all hostilities ceased. The spoiling of arms, at least during the battle, was also interdicted; and the consecration of the spoils of slain enemies to the gods, as, in general, all rejoicings for victory, were considered as ill-omened.'

Such was the war of the greatest soldiers who prayed to heathen gods. What Christian war is, preached by Christian ministers, let any one tell you, who saw the sacred crowning, and heard the sacred flute-playing, and was inspired and sanctified by the divinely-measured and musical language, of any North American regiment preparing for its charge. And what is the relative cost of life in

pagan and Christian wars, let this one fact tell you:—the
Spartans won the decisive battle of Corinth with the loss
of eight men; the victors at indecisive Gettysburg confess
to the loss of 30,000.

II. I pass now to our second order of war, the commonest
among men, that undertaken in desire of dominion. And
let me ask you to think for a few moments what the real
meaning of this desire of dominion is—first in the minds of
kings—then in that of nations.

Now, mind you this first,—that I speak either about kings,
or masses of men, with a fixed conviction that human nature
is a noble and beautiful thing; not a foul nor a base thing.
All the sin of men I esteem as their disease, not their nature;
as a folly which may be prevented, not a necessity which
must be accepted. And my wonder, even when things are
at their worst, is always at the height which this human
nature can attain. Thinking it high, I find it always a higher
thing than I thought it; while those who think it low, find
it, and will find it, always lower than they thought it: the
fact being, that it is infinite, and capable of infinite height
and infinite fall; but the nature of it—and here is the faith
which I would have you hold with me—the *nature* of it is in
the nobleness, not in the catastrophe.

Take the faith in its utmost terms. When the captain of
the 'London' shook hands with his mate, saying 'God speed

ƒou! I will go down with my passengers,' *that* I believe to
be 'human nature.' He does not do it from any religious
motive—from any hope of reward, or any fear of punishment; he does it because he is a man. But when a mother,
living among the fair fields of merry England, gives hei
two-year-old child to be suffocated under a mattress in hei
inner room, while the said mother waits and talks outside;
that I believe to be *not* human nature. You have the two
extremes there, shortly. And you, men, and mothers, who
are here face to face with me to-night, I call upon you to say
which of these is human, and which inhuman—which 'natural' and which 'unnatural?' Choose your creed at once, I
beseech you:—choose it with unshaken choice—choose it for
ever. Will you take, for foundation of act and hope, the
faith that this man was such as God made him, or that this
woman was such as God made her? Which of them has
failed from their nature—from their present, possible, actual
nature;—not their nature of long ago, but their nature of
now? Which has betrayed it—falsified it? Did the guar-
dian who died in his trust, die inhumanly, and as a fool; and
did the murderess of her child fulfil the law of her being?
Choose, I say; infinitude of choices hang upon this. You
have had false prophets among you—for centuries you have
had them—solemnly warned against them though you were;
false prophets, who have told you that all men are nothing

but fiends or wolves, half beast, half devil. Believe that, and indeed you may sink to that. But refuse that, and have faith that God 'made you upright,' though *you* have sought out many inventions; so, you will strive daily to become more what your Maker meant and means you to be, and daily gives you also the power to be—and you will cling more and more to the nobleness and virtue that is in you, saying, 'My righteousness I hold fast, and will not let it go.'

I have put this to you as a choice, as if you might hold either of these creeds you liked best. But there is in reality no choice for you; the facts being quite easily ascertainable. You have no business to *think* about this matter, or to choose in it. The broad fact is, that a human creature of the highest race, and most perfect as a human thing, is invariably both kind and true; and that as you lower the race, you get cruelty and falseness, as you get deformity: and this so steadily and assuredly, that the two great words which, in their first use, meant only perfection of race, have come, by consequence of the invariable connection of virtue with the fine human nature, both to signify benevolence of disposition. The word generous, and the word gentle, both, in their origin, meant only ' of pure race,' but because charity and tenderness are inseparable from this purity of blood, the words which once stood only for pride, now stand as synonyms for virtue.

Now, this being the true power of our inherent humanity,

and seeing that all the aim of education should be to develop this;—and seeing also what magnificent self sacrifice the higher classes of men are capable of, for any cause that they understand or feel,—it is wholly inconceivable to me how well-educated princes, who ought to be of all gentlemen the gentlest, and of all nobles the most generous, and whose title of royalty means only their function of doing every man '*right*'—how these, I say, throughout history, should so rarely pronounce themselves on the side of the poor and of justice, but continually maintain themselves and their own interests by oppression of the poor, and by wresting of justice; and how this should be accepted as so natural, that the word loyalty, which means faithfulness to law, is used as if it were only the duty of a people to be loyal to their king, and not the duty of a king to be infinitely more loyal to his people. How comes it to pass that a captain will die with his passengers, and lean over the gunwale to give the parting boat its course; but that a king will not usually die with, much less *for*, his passengers,—thinks it rather incumbent on his passengers, in any number, to die for *him?* Think, I beseech you, of the wonder of this. The sea captain, not captain by divine right, but only by company's appointment;—not a man of royal descent, but only a plebeian who can steer;—not with the eyes of the world upon him, but with feeble chance, depending on one poor boat, of his name being ever

5*

heard above the wash of the fatal waves;—not with the cause of a nation resting on his act, but helpless to save so much as a child from among the lost crowd with whom he resolves to be lost,—yet goes down quietly to his grave, rather than break his faith to these few emigrants. But your captain by divine right,—your captain with the hues of a hundred shields of kings upon his breast,—your captain whose every deed, brave or base, will be illuminated or branded for ever before unescapable eyes of men,—your captain whose every thought and act are beneficent, or fatal, from sunrising to setting, blessing as the sunshine, or shadowing as the night,—this captain, as you find him in history, for the most part thinks only how he may tax his passengers, and sit at most ease in his state cabin!

For observe, if there had been indeed in the hearts of the rulers of great multitudes of men any such conception of work for the good of those under their command, as there is in the good and thoughtful masters of any small company of men, not only wars for the sake of mere increase of power could never take place, but our idea of power itself would be entirely altered. Do you suppose that to think and act even for a million of men, to hear their complaints, watch their weaknesses, restrain their vices, make laws for them, lead them, day by day, to purer life, is not enough for one man's work? If any of us were absolute lord only of a district of

a hundred miles square, and were resolved on doing our utmost for it; making it feed as large a number of people as
possible; making every clod productive, and every rock
defensive, and every human being happy; should we not
have enough on our hands think you? But if the ruler has
any other aim than this; if, careless of the result of his inter-
ference, he desire only the authority to interfere; and, re-
gardless of what is ill-done or well-done, cares only that it
shall be done at his bidding;—if he would rather do two hundred miles' space of mischief, than one hundred miles' space of
good, of course he will try to add to his territory; and to add
illimitably. But does he add to his power? Do you call it
power in a child, if he is allowed to play with the wheels and
bands of some vast engine, pleased with their murmur and
whirl, till his unwise touch, wandering where it ought not,
scatters beam and wheel into ruin? Yet what machine is so
vast, so incognisable, as the working of the mind of a nation;
what child's touch so wanton, as the word of a selfish king?
And yet, how long have we allowed the historian to speak of
the extent of the calamity a man causes, as a just ground for
his pride; and to extol him as the greatest prince, who is
only the centre of the widest error. Follow out this thought
by yourselves; and you will find that all power, properly so
called, is wise and benevolent. There may be capacity in a
drifting fire-ship to destroy a fleet; there may be venom

enough in a dead body to infect a nation :—but which of you, the most ambitious, would desire a drifting kinghood, robed in consuming fire, or a poison-dipped sceptre whose touch was mortal ?   There is no true potency, remember, but that of help; nor true ambition, but ambition to save.

And then, observe farther, this true power, the power of saving, depends neither on multitude of men, nor on extent of territory.   We are continually assuming that nations become strong according to their numbers.   They indeed become so, if those numbers can be made of one mind; but how are you sure you can stay them in one mind, and keep them from having north and south minds ?   Grant them unanimous, how know you they will be unanimous in right ? If they are unanimous in wrong, the more they are, essentially the weaker they are.   Or, suppose that they can neither be of one mind, nor of two minds, but can only be of *no* mind ?   Suppose they are a mere helpless mob; tottering into precipitant catastrophe, like a waggon load of stones when the wheel comes off.   Dangerous enough for their neighbours, certainly, but not 'powerful.'

Neither does strength depend on extent of territory, any more than upon number of population.   Take up your maps when you go home this evening,—put the cluster of British Isles beside the mass of South America; and then consider whether any race of men need care how much ground they

stand upon. The strength is in the men, and in their unity
and virtue, not in their standing room: a little group of wise
hearts is better than a wilderness full of fools; and only that
nation gains true territory, which gains itself.

And now for the brief practical outcome of all this. Re
member, no government is ultimately strong, but in proportion to its kindness and justice; and that a nation does not
strengthen, by merely multiplying and diffusing itself. We
have not strengthened as yet, by multiplying into America.
Nay, even when it has not to encounter the separating conditions of emigration, a nation need not boast itself of multiplying on its own ground, if it multiplies only as flies or locusts
do, with the god of flies for its god. It multiplies its strength
only by increasing as one great family, in perfect fellowship
and brotherhood. And lastly, it does not strengthen itself
by seizing dominion over races whom it cannot benefit.
Austria is not strengthened, but weakened, by her grasp of
Lombardy; and whatever apparent increase of majesty and
of wealth may have accrued to us from the possession of
India, whether these prove to us ultimately power or weakness, depends wholly on the degree in which our influence on
the native race shall be benevolent and exalting. But, as it
is at their own peril that any race extends their dominion in
mere desire of power, so it is at their own still greater peril
that they refuse to undertake aggressive war, according to

their force, whenever they are assured that their authority would be helpful and protective. Nor need you listen to any sophistical objection of the impossibility of knowing when a people's help is needed, or when not. Make your national conscience clean, and your national eyes will soon be clear. No man who is truly ready to take part in a noble quarrel will ever stand long in doubt by whom, or in what cause, his aid is needed. I hold it my duty to make no political statement of any special bearing in this presence; but I tell you broadly and boldly, that, within these last ten years, we English have, as a knightly nation, lost our spurs: we have fought where we should not have fought, for gain; and we have been passive where we should not have been passive, for fear. I tell you that the principle of non-intervention, as now preached among us, is as selfish and cruel as the worst frenzy of conquest, and differs from it only by being not only malignant, but dastardly.

I know, however, that my opinions on this subject differ too widely from those ordinarily held, to be any farther intruded upon you; and therefore I pass lastly to examine the conditions of the third kind of noble war;—war waged simply for defence of the country in which we were born, and for the maintenance and execution of her laws, by whomsoever threatened or defied. It is to this duty that I suppose most men entering the army consider themselves in reality to be bound, and I want you now to reflect what the laws of mere defence are; and what the soldier's duty, as now understood, or supposed to be understood. You have solemnly devoted your selves to be English soldiers, for the guardianship of England. I want you to feel what this vow of yours indeed means, or is gradually coming to mean. You take it upon you, first, while you are sentimental schoolboys; you go into your military convent, or barracks, just as a girl goes into her convent while she is a sentimental schoolgirl; neither of you then know what you are about, though both the good soldiers and good nuns make the best of it afterwards. You don't understand perhaps why I call you 'sentimental' schoolboys, when you go into the army? Because, on the whole, it is love of adventure, of excitement, of fine dress and of the pride of fame, all which are sentimental motives, which chiefly make a boy like going into the Guards better than into a counting-house. You fancy, perhaps, that there is a severe sense of duty mixed with these peacocky motives? And in the best of you, there is; but do not think that it is principal. If you cared to do your duty to your country in a prosaic and unsentimental way, depend upon it, there is now truer duty to be done in raising harvests, than in burning them; more in building houses, than in shelling them—more in winning money by your own work, wherewith to help men, than in taxing other people's work, for money wherewith to slay men; more duty finally, in honest and unselfish living than in honest and unselfish dying, though that seems to your boys' eyes the bravest. So far then, as for your own honour, and the honour of your families, you choose brave death in a red coat before brave life in a black one, you are sentimental; and now see what this passionate vow of yours comes to. For a little while you ride, and you hunt tigers or savages, you shoot, and are shot; you are happy, and proud, always, and honoured and wept if you die; and you are satisfied with your life, and with the end of it; believing, on the whole, that good rather than harm of it comes to others, and much pleasure to you. But as the sense of duty enters into your forming minds, the vow takes another aspect. You find that you have put yourselves into the hand of your country as a weapon. You have vowed to strike, when she bids you, and to stay scabbarded when she bids you; all that you need answer for is, that you fail not in her grasp. And there is goodness in this, and greatness, if you can trust the hand and heart of the Britomart who has braced you to her side, and are assured that when she leaves you sheathed in darkness, there is no need for your flash to the sun. But remember, good and noble as this state may be, it is a state of slavery. There are different kinds of slaves and different masters. Some slaves are scourged to their work by whips, others are scourged to it by restlessness or ambition. It does not matter what the whip is; it is none the less a whip, because you have cut thongs for it out of your own souls: the fact, so far, of slavery, is in being driven to your work without thought, at another's bidding. Again, some slaves are bought with money, and others with praise. It matters not what the purchase-money is. The distinguishing sign of slavery is to have a price, and be bought for it. Again, it matters not what kind of work you are set on; some slaves are set to forced diggings, others to forced marches; some dig furrows, others field-works, and others graves. Some press the juice of reeds, and some the juice of vines, and some the blood of men. The fact of the captivity is the same whatever work we are set upon, though the fruits of the toil may be different. But, remember, in thus vowing ourselves to be the slaves of any master, it ought to be some subject of forethought with us, what work he is likely to put us upon. You may think that the whole duty of a soldier is to be passive, that it is the country you have left behind who is to command, and you have only to obey. But are you sure that you have left *all* your country behind, or that the part of it you have so left is indeed the best part of it? Suppose—and, remember, it is quite conceivable—that you yourselves are indeed the best part of England; that you, who have become the slaves, ought to have been the masters; and that those who are the masters, ought to have been the slaves! If it is a noble and whole-hearted England, whose bidding you are bound to do, it is well; but if you are yourselves the best of her heart, and the England you have left be but a half-hearted England, how say you of your obedience? You were too proud to become shopkeepers: are you satisfied then to become the servants of shopkeepers? You were too proud to become merchants or farmers yourselves: will you have merchants or farmers then for your field marshals? You had no gifts of special grace for Exeter Hall: will you have some gifted person thereat for your commander-in-chief, to judge of your work, and reward it? You imagine yourselves to be the army of England: how if you should find yourselves, at last, only the police of her manufacturing towns, and the beadles of her little Bethels?

It is not so yet, nor will be so, I trust, for ever; but what I want you to see, and to be assured of, is, that the ideal of soldiership is not mere passive obedience and bravery; that, so far from this, no country is in a healthy state which has separated, even in a small degree, her civil from her military power. All states of the world, however great, fall at once when they use mercenary armies; and although it is a less instant form of error (because involving no national taint of cowardice), it is yet an error no less ultimately fatal—it is the error especially of modern times, of which we cannot yet know all the calamitous consequences—to take away the best blood and strength of the nation, all the soul-substance of it that is brave, and careless of reward, and scornful of pain, and faithful in trust; and to cast that into steel, and make a mere sword of it; taking away its voice and will; but to keep the worst part of the nation—whatever is cowardly, avaricious, sensual, and faithless—and to give to this the voice, to this the authority, to this the chief privilege, where there is least capacity, of thought. The fulfilment of your vow for the defence of England will by no means consist in carrying out such a system. You are not true soldiers, if you only mean to stand at a shop door, to protect shop-boys who are cheating inside. A soldier's vow to his country is that he will die for the guardianship of her domestic virtue, of her righteous laws, and of her anyway challenged or endangered honour. A state without virtue, without laws, and without honour, he is bound *not* to defend; nay, bound to redress by his own right hand that which he sees to be base in her. So sternly is this the law of Nature and life, that a nation once utterly corrupt can only be redeemed by a military despotism—never by talking, nor by its free effort. And the health of any state consists simply in this: that in it, those who are wisest shall also be strongest; its rulers should be also its soldiers; or, rather, by force of intellect more than of sword, its soldiers its rulers. Whatever the hold which the aristocracy of England has on the heart of England, in that they are still always in front of her battles, this hold will not be enough, unless they are also in front of her thoughts. And truly her thoughts need good captain's eading now, if ever! Do you know what, by this beautiful division of labour (her brave men fighting, and her cowards thinking), she has come at last to think? Here is a bit of paper in my hand,* a good one too, and an honest one; quite representative of the best common public thought of England at this moment; and it is holding forth in one of its leaders upon our 'social welfare,'—upon our 'vivid life'—upon the 'political supremacy of Great Britain.'

* I do not care to refer to the journal quoted, because the article was unworthy of its general tone, though in order to enable the audience to verify the quoted sentence, I left the number containing it on the table, when I delivered this lecture. But a saying of Baron Liebig's, quoted at the head of a leader on the same subject in the 'Daily Telegraph' of January 11, 1866, summarily digests and presents the maximum folly of modern thought in this respect. 'Civilization,' says the Baron, 'is the economy of power, and English power is coal.' Not altogether so, my chemical friend. Civilization is the making of civil persons, which is a kind of distillation of which alembics are incapable, and does not at all imply the turning of a small company of gentlemen into a large company of ironmongers. And English power (what little of it may be left), is by no means coal, but, indeed, of that which, 'when the whole world turns to coal, then chiefly lives.'

And what do you think all these are owing to? To what
our English sires have done for us, and taught us, age after
age? No: not to that. To our honesty of heart, or cool-
ness of head, or steadiness of will? No: not to these. To
our thinkers, or our statesmen, or our poets, or our captains, or our martyrs, or the patient labour of our poor?
No: not to these; or at least not to these in any chief
measure. Nay, says the journal, 'more than any agency,
it is the cheapness and abundance of our coal which have
made us what we are.' If it be so, then 'ashes to ashes'
be our epitaph! and the sooner the better. I tell you,
gentlemen of England, if ever you would have your country
breathe the pure breath of heaven again, and receive again a
soul into her body, instead of rotting into a carcase, blown
up in the belly with carbonic acid (and great *that* way), you
must think, and feel, for your England, as well as fight for
her: you must teach her that all the true greatness she
ever had, or ever can have, she won while her fields were
green and her faces ruddy;—that greatness is still possible
for Englishmen, even though the ground be not hollow
under their feet, nor the sky black over their heads;—and
that, when the day comes for their country to lay her
honours in the dust, her crest will not rise from it more
loftily because it is dust of coal. Gentlemen, I tell you,
solemnly, that the day is coming when the soldiers of

England must be her tutors; and the captains of her army, captains also of her mind.

And now, remember, you soldier youths, who are, thus in all ways the hope of your country; or must be, if she have any hope: remember that your fitness for all future trust depends upon what you are now. No good soldier in his old age was ever careless or indolent in his youth. Many a giddy and thoughtless boy has become a good bishop, or a good lawyer, or a good merchant; but no such an one ever became a good general. I challenge you, in all history, to find a record of a good soldier who was not grave and earnest in his youth. And, in general, I have no patience with people who talk about 'the thoughtlessness of youth' indulgently. I had infinitely rather hear of thoughtless old age, and the indulgence due to *that*. When a man has done his work, and nothing can any way be materially altered in his fate, let him forget his toil, and jest with his fate, if he will; but what excuse can you find for wilfulness of thought, at the very time when every crisis of future fortune hangs on your decisions? A youth thoughtless! when all the happiness of his home for ever depends on the chances, or the passions, of an hour! A youth thoughtless! when the career of all his days depends on the opportunity of a moment! A youth thoughtless! when his every act is a foundation-stone of future conduct,

and every imagination a fountain of life or death! Be
thoughtless in *any* after years, rather than now—though,
indeed, there is only one place where a man may be nobly
thoughtless,—his deathbed. No thinking should ever be
left to be done there.

Having, then, resolved that you will not waste recklessly,
but earnestly use, these early days of yours, remember that
all the duties of her children to England may be summed
in two words—industry, and honour. I say first, industry,
for it is in this that soldier youth are especially tempted to
fail. Yet, surely, there is no reason, because your life may
possibly or probably be shorter than other men's, that you
should therefore waste more recklessly the portion of it
that is granted you; neither do the duties of your profession, which require you to keep your bodies strong, in any
wise involve the keeping of your minds weak. So far
from that, the experience, the hardship, and the activity
of a soldier's life render his powers of thought more accu
rate than those of other men; and while, for others, all
knowledge is often little more than a means of amusement,
there is no form of science which a soldier may not at
some time or other find bearing on business of life and
death. A young mathematician may be excused for lan-
guor in studying curves to be described only with a pen-
cil; but not in tracing those which are to be described

with a rocket. Your knowledge of a wholesome herb may
involve the feeding of an army; and acquaintance with an
obscure point of geography, the success of a campaign.
Never waste an instant's time, therefore; the sin of idleness is a thousand-fold greater in you than in other
youths; for the fates of those who will one day be under
your command hang upon your knowledge; lost moments
now will be lost lives then, and every instant which you
carelessly take for play, you buy with blood. But there is
one way of wasting time, of all the vilest, because it wastes,
not time only, but the interest and energy of your minds.
Of all the ungentlemanly habits into which you can fall,
the vilest is betting, or interesting yourselves in the issues
of betting. It unites nearly every condition of folly and
vice; you concentrate your interest upon a matter of chance,
instead of upon a subject of true knowledge; and you back
opinions which you have no grounds for forming, merely
because they are your own. All the insolence of egotism
is in this; and so far as the love of excitement is compli-
cated with the hope of winning money, you turn yourselves
into the basest sort of tradesmen—those who live by specu-
lation. Were there no other ground for industry, this
would be a sufficient one; that it protected you from the
temptation to so scandalous a vice. Work faithfully, and
you will put yourselves in possession of a glorious and en-

larging happiness; not such as can be won by the speed of a horse, or marred by the obliquity of a ball.

First, then, by industry you must fulfil your vow to your country; but all industry and earnestness will be useless unless they are consecrated by your resolution to be in all things men of honour; not honour in the common sense only, but in the highest. Rest on the force of the two main words in the great verse, *integer* vitæ, scelerisque *purus*. You have vowed your life to England; give it her wholly—a bright, stainless, perfect life—a knightly life. Because you have to fight with machines instead of lances, there may be a necessity for more ghastly danger, but there is none for less worthiness of character, than in olden time. You may be true knights yet, though perhaps not *equites ;* you may have to call yourselves 'cannonry' instead of 'chivalry,' but that is no reason why you should not call yourselves true men. So the first thing you have to see to in becoming soldiers is that you make yourselves wholly true. Courage is a mere matter of course among any ordinarily well-born youths; but neither truth nor gentleness is matter of course. You must bind them like shields about your necks; you must write them on the tables of your hearts. Though it be not exacted of you, yet exact it of yourselves, this vow of stainless truth. Your hearts are, if you leave them unstirred, as tombs in which a god lies buried. Vow yourselves crusaders to redeem that sacred sepulchre. And remember, before all things—for no other memory will be so protective of you—that the highest law of this knightly truth is that under which it is vowed to women. Whomsoever else you deceive, whomsoever you injure, whomsoever you leave unaided, you must not deceive, nor injure, nor leave unaided, according to your power, any woman of whatever rank. Believe me, every virtue of the higher phases of manly character begins in this;—in truth and modesty before the face of all maidens; in truth and pity, or truth and reverence, to all womanhood.

And now let me turn for a moment to you,—wives and maidens, who are the souls of soldiers; to you,—mothers, who have devoted your children to the great hierarchy of war. Let me ask you to consider what part you have to take for the aid of those who love you; for if you fail in your part they cannot fulfil theirs; such absolute helpmates you are that no man can stand without that help, nor labour in his own strength.

I know your hearts, and that the truth of them never fails when an hour of trial comes which you recognise for such. But you know not when the hour of trial first finds you, nor when it verily finds you. You imagine that you are only called upon to wait and to suffer; to surrender and to mourn. You know that you must not weaken the hearts of your husbands and lovers, even by the one fear of which those hearts are capable,—the fear of parting from you, or of causing you grief. Through weary years of separation· through fearful expectancies of unknown fate; through the tenfold bitterness of the sorrow which might so easily have been joy, and the tenfold yearning for glorious life struck down in its prime—through all these agonies you fail not, and never will fail. But your trial is not in these. To be heroic in danger is little;—you are Englishwomen. To be heroic in change and sway of fortune is little;—for do you not love? To be patient through the great chasm and pause of loss is little;—for do you not still love in heaven? But to be heroic in happiness; to bear yourselves gravely and right-eously in the dazzling of the sunshine of morning; not to forget the God in whom you trust, when He gives you most; not to fail those who trust you, when they seem to need you least; this is the difficult fortitude. It is not in the pining of absence, not in the peril of battle, not in the wasting of sickness, that your prayer should be most passionate, or your guardianship most tender. Pray, mothers and maidens, for your young soldiers in the bloom of their pride; pray for them, while the only dangers round them are in their own wayward wills; watch you, and pray, when they have to face, not death, but temptation. But it is this fortitude also for which there is the crowning reward. Believe me, the whole course and character of your lovers' lives is in your hands; what you would have them be, they shall be, if you not only desire to have them so, but deserve to have them so ; for they are but mirrors in which you will see yourselves imaged. If you are frivolous, they will be so also ; if you have no understanding of the scope of their duty, they also will forget it ; they will listen,—they *can* listen,—to no other interpretation of it than that uttered from your lips. Bid them be brave ;—they will be brave for you ; bid them be cowards ; and how noble soever they be ;—they will quail for you. Bid them be wise, and they will be wise for you ; mock at their counsel, they will be fools for you : such and so absolute is your rule over them. You fancy, perhaps, as you have been told so often, that a wife's rule should only be over her husband's house, not over his mind. Ah, no ! the true rule is just the reverse of that ; a true wife, in her husband's house, is his servant ; it is in his heart that she is queen. Whatever of the best he can conceive, it is her part to be ; whatever of highest he can hope, it is hers to promise ; all that is dark in him she must purge into purity ; all that is failing in him she must strengthen into truth : from her, through all the world's clamour, he must win his praise ; in her, through all the world's warfare, he must find his peace.

And, now, but one word more. You may wonder, per-haps, that I have spoken all this night in praise of war

Yet, truly, if it might be, I, for one, would fain join in the
cadence of hammer-strokes that should beat swords into
ploughshares: and that this cannot be, is not the fault of us
men. It is *your* fault. Wholly yours. Only by your command, or by your permission, can any contest take place
among us. And the real, final, reason for all the poverty,
misery, and rage of battle, throughout Europe, is simply that
you women, however good, however religious, however self-
sacrificing for those whom you love, are too selfish and too
thoughtless to take pains for any creature out of your own
immediate circles. You fancy that you are sorry for the
pain of others. Now I just tell you this, that if the usual
course of war, instead of unroofing peasants' houses, and
ravaging peasants' fields, merely broke the china upon your
own drawing-room tables, no war in civilised countries
would last a week. I tell you more, that at whatever
moment you chose to put a period to war, you could do it
with less trouble than you take any day to go out to dinner.
You know, or at least you might know if you would think,
that every battle you hear of has made many widows and
orphans. We have, none of us, heart enough truly to mourn
with these. But at least we might put on the outer symbols
of mourning with them. Let but every Christian lady who
has conscience toward God, vow that she will mourn, at least
outwardly, for His killed creatures. Your praying is use-

less, and your churchgoing mere mockery of God, if you have not plain obedience in you enough for this. Let every lady in the upper classes of civilised Europe simply vow that, while any cruel war proceeds, she will wear *black;*—a mute's black,—with no jewel, no ornament, no excuse for, or evasion into, prettiness.—I tell you again, no war would last a week.

And lastly. You women of England are all now shrieking with one voice,—you and your clergymen together,—because you hear of your Bibles being attacked. If you choose to obey your Bibles, you will never care who attacks them. It is just because you never fulfil a single downright precept of the Book, that you are so careful for its credit: and just because you don't care to obey its whole words, that you are so particular about the letters of them. The Bible tells you to dress plainly,—and you are mad for finery; the Bible tells you to have pity on the poor,—and you crush them under your carriage-wheels; the Bible tells you to do judgment and justice,—and you do not know, nor care to know, so much as what the Bible word 'justice means' Do but learn so much of God's truth as that comes to; know what He means when He tells you to be just: and teach your sons, that their bravery is but a fool's boast, and their deeds but a firebrand's tossing, unless they are indeed Just men, and Perfect in the Fear of God;—and you will soon have no more war, unless it be indeed such as is willed by Him, of whom, though Prince of Peace, it is also written, 'In Righteousness He doth judge, and make war.'

THE END.

www.ingramcontent.com/pod-product-compliance
Lightning Source LLC
Chambersburg PA
CBHW030905050726
47500CB00009B/1025